TRAPPED

The shots came closer than any so far to nailing Clay Taggart. Two whizzed past his cheek. The third smacked into the dirt inches above his head. Clay paid them no heed. He had spotted the officer in charge of the patrol. Hastily aligning his sights, he held his breath a moment, then stroked the trigger.

When Taggart ran out of targets, he spied a wide cleft nearby and threw himself into it as a ragged volley peppered the bench. Then the volley faded, and he peeked about the rim. The troopers were swiftly ringing the bluff. In another minute they would have it surrounded.

He was trapped.

8

WHITE APACHE

THE TRACKERS

Jake McMasters

LEISURE BOOKS **NEW YORK CITY**

To Judy, Joshua, and Shane.

A LEISURE BOOK®

August 1995

Published by

Dorchester Publishing Co., Inc.
276 Fifth Avenue
New York, NY 10001

Printed in the United States of America.

Chapter One

The pale glare of a full moon bathed the stark Arizona landscape. Deep in the Gila Mountains, upthrust spires of rock clawed at the sky as if striving to tear the lunar eye from its socket.

Over a rocky ridge clattered three shod horses. The animals had been pushed to the limits of their endurance. All of them were caked thick with sweat. They rasped like steam engines when the men astride them hauled on the reins to stop and look back.

There was a grim air about the men. Their movements were jerky and quick, as if they were highstrung. Their whites faces seemed much paler than even the moonlight would allow. It lent them the aspect of living ghosts.

"Do you think we lost them?" asked the stockiest of the trio in a New England accent. Like his companions, he wore a dusty uniform. Anyone familiar with the military would have known at a glance that Pvt. Earl Fetterman was a trooper in the Fifth Cavalry of the United States Army. Or he had been, at any rate, until early that very morning.

"Of course we did," snapped the tallest of the three. "No one can track us over ground that hard." Pvt. William Stillwell was from Florida. More than anything else in life, he missed being able to take a stroll on the beach and diving into the surf as the whim struck him. That, and a certain young woman named Darcy who had promised to wait forever but who was now seeing his best friend. His *former* best friend.

The third man made a sound like a bobcat choking on a bone. "Idiots!" he snarled. Pvt. James Koch was from New York City, which everyone claimed had a lot to do with his chronic sour temper. "Don't you know not to take anything for granted? I say we don't rest easy until we reach Denver." His bay bobbed its head, nearly pulling the reins from his grasp. Hissing, Koch slapped it. "Hell, I won't relax until I'm back in Queens where I belong. I must have been crazy to dream of joining the Army."

"We all were," Earl agreed.

The young man from Florida shrugged. "Live and learn, as I always say." Stillwell clucked to his sorrel. "Now let's keep going. We have to stay on schedule. By morning we should reach the Salt River."

Earl Fetterman nodded and licked his thick lips. "Provided the horses don't play out on us. If you ask me, we've been pushing them too damn hard."

Pvt. Koch snorted as he fell into place behind Stillwell. "What do you know about horses, Bean Boy? You never rode one until you enlisted, just like the rest of us."

"Don't call me that, friend," Earl bristled. "I

6

don't like having anyone poke fun at my home town."

Koch's brittle laugh tinkled on the brisk breeze as the three young soldiers raced northward. Pvt. Fetterman did not mind bringing up the rear. That way he did not have to put up with Koch's constant smirk or Stillwell's steady glare.

Earl felt sorry for the latter. From the first day they met at Fort Bowie, Stillwell had been a happy, carefree fellow. All Stillwell had talked about was the beautiful girl waiting for him in Jacksonville. Stillwell even had a tiny photograph which he kept in a locket worn around his neck. And if the man had shown that picture to Earl once, he had shown it to him a hundred times. It had gotten to the point where Earl half swore that he knew Darcy Thompson's features better than he did his own sister's.

Then Stillwell had gotten that awful letter. The poor man had been all torn up inside. He had ranted and raved and clutched the locket to his chest as if his heart were about to burst.

Earl had never seen anyone so upset. He supposed that he should not have been very surprised when Stillwell first mentioned desertion, but he had been. Even though all of them hated the Army, even though all of them wished they had never taken the oath, none of them had ever voiced the idea uppermost on all their minds. Until Stillwell did.

It had amazed Earl to hear anyone talk that way. It had astounded him even more when Koch had chimed in that he was interested. And before Earl quite knew how it happened, he had startled himself by agreeing to go along.

The truth was that Army life did not suit Earl one bit. He heartily disliked having to get up before the

7

crack of dawn each and every day. He detested the many hours spent at hard labor and on parade. He loathed the boredom of guard duty. And he absolutely despised the Army's excuse for food.

Earl Fetterman had been raised in Boston by caring parents. They cared so much that often when he was small they would do his school homework for him to spare him the torment of having to wrestle with problems he was too young to understand. They cared so much that his mother kept his room as neat as a pin without him ever having to lift a finger to help. They cared so much that his father had not made Earl come down to the family business on the docks to help out until Earl was 15, and then all Earl had to do was sit in the office and help oversee operations.

Earl had to admit that he had never quite realized how good he had it until he entered the Army. He fondly recalled the many times his mother had let him sleep in until noon. He remembered all too well the delicious meals she would make for him at any time of the day or night. And his father! How the man had loved to take Earl hunting and fishing and to the races!

Those were the days, Earl fondly mused. He had been a fool to dream of more, a fool to read those trashy penny dreadfuls and to get so fired up with thoughts of adventure and excitement that he had gone downtown and enlisted without first consulting his parents.

It had been the single greatest mistake of his life.

But now it was behind him! Earl squared his sloped shoulders and held his head high. He was saying goodbye to Army life forever. Once he was safely back in Boston, he would never leave again. His father was a man of some influence and should be able to secure a discharge without too much trouble. It was widely known that certain high-ranking officers would take money under the table in that regard. Within a month Earl would be right where he belonged, at his desk on the docks, telling the longshoremen how to unload and load ships. Earl could hardly wait.

Suddenly the night was rent by a wavering howl. Earl slowed and called out, "Did you hear that?"

Koch answered without turning. "It's another damn coyote. We must have heard fifty in the past hour alone. Don't wet yourself over it."

Earl did not reply. He resented the insult, but that was just Koch being Koch. As for the howl, he was sure that it was much different than those he had heard earlier, much different than any howl he had ever heard except maybe one.

Earl thought back to the time he had been on guard duty and a wolf had howled near the fort. The old scout, Sieber, had snickered when he had nearly jumped out of his skin and told him not to worry, that wolves were getting scarce in those parts and that they hardly ever bothered a person and certainly had never been known to band together to attack forts. Earl had known the old scout was having fun at his expense, but he hadn't minded. Sieber was a likable character who knew more wonderful stories than any man alive.

That howl, though, had stuck with Earl. Every now and again he remembered it. Usually late at night when he was making the rounds of the horses or on camp perimeter duty. That howl, Earl believed, had been a lot like the one he had just heard.

Still, Earl was not very worried. Wolves did not attack humans. Sieber had said as much. And even if they did, there were three of them and they all had revolvers and carbines. They could hold a pack of wolves at bay.

Presently another howl rent the night. This one was much closer. Earl twisted in the saddle to regard the bleak terrain they had crossed. It was almost as if the wolf were following them, an absurd idea.

Or was it?

What if it wasn't a wolf?

What if it was something else? Something much worse?

What if they were being trailed by Indians?

The terrifying thought made a tingle of raw fear shoot down Earl's spine. He had heard tales, too many to count. Tales of how Indians could imitate any animal alive. Tales of how the savages often yipped like coyotes and wolves to fool those they stalked. Tales of how Indians could slip up on a man without him knowing and slit his throat in the blink of an eye.

The very worst Indians, of course, were the Apaches. The mere mention of the name was enough to make Earl break out in goosebumps. Everyone knew that Apaches were vicious killers who took delight in ripping hearts from living victims. Older soldiers had told Earl all about the many massacres, and every gory detail of every horrible raid Apaches ever committed.

It did not matter at all to Earl that the old scout, Sieber, branded many of their tales as outright lies. It did not mean a thing to him that Sieber claimed Indians in general, and Apaches in particular, were no better or worse than white people. Earl knew better. He just knew.

Earl anxiously scanned the jagged southern horizon. Nothing moved that he could see, but that did not mean much. It was said that Apaches could sneak up on a man in an open field in broad daylight and never be caught. It was said that they knew how to turn invisible at will.

The very worst of them, Earl had been told, were the renegades. Most Apaches were now on reservations, either at San Carlos or the Chiricahua Reservation. But the renegades refused to go to either place. They refused to give up the old ways.

Sieber had told Earl why. The renegades did not think the government had the right to tell people where to live. The renegades did not want the government to feed them and clothe them, or doctor them when they were sick. The renegades saw the government as a great fat spider trying to suck the lifeblood from their people, and they hated the government for it.

Frankly, Earl did not see why they were so upset. It had always been nice to have his parents do for him, so the Apaches should be just as grateful to have the government look after them. But there was just no pleasing some people.

Especially not the very worst of all the renegades, a small band led by the traitor called the White Apache. More stories were told about him than about anyone else. The man had been a rancher once, but turned his back on white ways after he was caught trying to force himself on a neighbor's wife. Now he butchered and raped and pillaged to his heart's content, and no one seemed able to stop him.

Sieber had claimed to know Taggart back in the days before the bloodshed began. The scout had taken an oath on the fact that Clay Taggart had been as decent as the day was long. Sieber suspected there was more to the story of Taggart's

11

turning traitor than was common knowledge.

Be that as it may, Earl was not about to let the traitor, or any other Apache, get their hands on him. He checked the back trail many times over the next half an hour. Not once did he see any cause for alarm, although he did hear the strange howl twice more and each time it was closer than the time before.

Shortly after midnight, Stillwell suddenly let out with an oath and drew rein. Koch stopped next to him on the right, so Earl swung to the left.

"What's wrong?"

The young man from Florida slid off his mount and sank to one knee to examine a front leg. "I can't believe my luck!" Stillwell snapped. "I think my damn horse is going lame." He roughly ran a hand over the fetlock and the knee as he had been taught and wanted to scream in frustration when he found the leg to be slightly swollen. Nothing had gone right for him since the day he received the letter from Darcy.

"Is it?" Jim Koch asked, not out of concern for Stillwell. He was thinking of himself, and the fact that he was not about to let Stillwell ride double with him and maybe ruin his own chances of reaching safety.

"Afraid so." The lovesick Floridian stood and gestured in disgust. "Now what do we do? I sure as hell can't walk all the way to Denver."

Koch had a ready answer. "If the dumb brute is going to give out on you anyway, you might as well ride it until it drops. Then we'll make up our minds what to do."

Stillwell nodded. It made sense to him. Grabbing the saddle horn, he wearily swung up. "Just don't

12

push too hard," he advised. "This nag will last longer that way."

Abruptly, to their rear, a wavering howl shattered the crisp night air. Earl spun around so fast that he nearly fell off his horse. He tried to claw his revolver out but fumbled at the heavy flap.

Koch snickered. "There you go again, Bean Boy. Scared of a stupid coyote."

"It's not, I tell you!" Earl held his ground. The short hairs at the nape of his neck prickled as he scoured the arid tract behind them. He had the oddest feeling that unseen eyes were on them.

"What else could it be?" Koch asked, his tone so sarcastic it could have been cut with a knife. "Apaches? None of the tame ones would dare bother us. As for the renegades, Cpl. Baird told us that recent reports have them south of the border, raiding in Mexico."

"Maybe those reports were wrong," Earl insisted. An idea hit him, and he snapped his fingers. "I know! It could be old Seiber and the Apache scouts! They came back earlier than we expected and the colonel sent them to bring us in."

Koch rolled his eyes skyward. He never had thought highly of Fetterman and had only agreed to count him in because Stillwell liked him. "How many times do I have to tell you? I had Orderly Duty yesterday. I know for a fact that every last scout is down in the Dragoons. Seiber and those red devils who work with him were sent to help catch a pair of bucks who skipped from San Carlos." Koch shook his head. "The scouts won't be back at Fort Bowie for a week or so yet. So quit getting in a huff over every little sound, Bean Boy."

Earl held his tongue as the other two rode out. He followed, sulking. All Koch ever did was treat him as if he were ten years old, and he had grown to resent it highly. In his opinion, Jim Koch was no better than he was. Both of them had been as green as grass, as Sieber would say, when they were sent to that godforsaken country.

It made Earl happy to be leaving Arizona Territory for good. The idea that any sane soul would want to live there stunned him. Not when so many places were so much nicer. Massachusetts, for instance, did not have a climate that roasted a man as if he were in an oven in the summer and froze him as if he were encased in solid ice in the winter. Massachusetts had four seasons, not just two.

There was plenty of water in Earl's home state, as well. A man did not have to worry about dying of thirst every time he strayed into the wilderness. Nor did a man have to worry about gila monsters, scorpions or sidewinders.

All in all, Earl Fetterman considered Arizona the single most hostile environment on the face of the planet. It was small wonder the Apaches were as hard as they were, he reflected. Hard land bred hard men. Earl had promised himself that he would never set foot there again for as long as he lived.

The next moment Earl's train of thought was derailed by a low growl behind him. Shocked, he turned, his right hand falling to the butt of his pistol. That he had only practiced with it a half-dozen times and could not hit the broad side of a barracks at 20 paces did not seem to bother him. He started to draw but stopped when he saw no hint of movement anywhere. Yet he was certain that he had heard an animal.

From then on, Earl rode twisted in the saddle so he could keep an eye on what was in front of them and what lay to their rear. Tense minutes dragged by.

Without warning, a vague figure dashed between two high boulders, vanishing in the blink of an eye.

Earl let out with a squawk and reined up. He drew his revolver, his thumb resting on the hammer. His companions joined him, and Koch was none too pleased.

"What the hell is it this time, Bean Boy? Haven't you tried our patience enough? Are you going to act like this all the way to Denver?"

Keeping his voice as calm as he could, Earl said, "I saw someone."

"You saw nothing!" Koch challenged. "You're a simpleton who is letting his imagination get the better of him!"

Pvt. Bill Stillwill coughed. "Now hold on, Jim. There is no need for you to fly off the handle. Earl is a good man or we wouldn't have brought him along. If he says he saw something, then by God he must have seen something."

"Not something," Earl corrected, "someone. We're being stalked, I tell you."

Koch sneered and muttered, "Here we go again."

Scowling at the New Yorker, Stillwell nudged his horse past theirs and rose in the stirrups to study the tableland they were traversing. "I don't see a thing, Earl. Is Jim right? Could you have been mistaken?"

As if in answer there came a sharp whistling sound and then a loud thump as a fist might make striking human flesh. Neither Earl nor Koch knew the cause and glanced at once another in confusion.

"Bill?" Earl asked Stillwell. "Did you hear that strange noise?"

The trooper from Florida shifted around as if to

answer but no words came out of his gaping mouth. What did come out was a pathetic sort of whine which tapered in a gurgled grunt of utter torment and amazement all rolled into one. His right hand lifted as if to salute but stopped short at his chest where the feathered end of a long shaft jutted out. Blood spurted from the corners of his mouth and out his nose. He attempted to raise his hand higher, to the heart-shaped gold locket around his neck, but the effort sapped what little life he had left and his whole body seemed to melt inward on itself, then oozed to the ground in a miserable disjointed heap.

"Sweet Jesus!" Koch breathed.

From the top of a flat boulder a dozen yards away wafted a high cackle. "Hell, boy! The Good Lord had nothin' to do with it. You done brought this on yourselves. With the scouts gone, that Yankee, Petersen, had to send us to fetch you. And we don't fetch but one way. Over a saddle."

Pvt. Koch glanced up and wet himself. He had been posted at Bowie longer than the other two. He knew the identity of the buckskin clad scarecrow on the boulder and knew they were as good as dead. But knowing that fact did not stop him from doing something about it.

James Koch had a number of traits which annoyed his fellow soldiers no end. But not one of those who knew him had ever seen fit to brand him a coward. Even Koch's desertion did not stem from cowardice. He was giving up Army life because he hated having others tell him what to do all the time. It was as simple as that. He would never have joined in the first place if a certain New York judge had given him any choice.

Now, wheeling his horse, Koch knew that his

16

choices in life had narrowed to two; live or die. He took off like the proverbial bat out of hell. He swept past Fetterman and flashed across a clearing toward more boulders. If he reached them, if he put them at his back to ward off arrows and bullets, he felt he might have a chance.

Then another buckskin clad form seemed to rise up out of nowhere in front of him. Too late, Koch saw the peculiar raccoon cap and the short blonde hair and knew that he had blundered into the worst of the bunch. In sheer desperation he went for his pistol. But compared to the killer, his movements were the speed of petrified molasses.

The apparition in the coonskin cap leveled an old Sharps and fired. The .52-caliber breechloader was powerful enough to drop a charging bull buffalo at that range. Pvt. William Koch was lifted clear out of the saddle by the impact and flung over a dozen feet to crash onto his side on the rocks.

Earl Fetterman felt his stomach churn. He sat there paralyzed, unable to move even though his mind shrieked at him to ride as he had never ridden before. "Oh, God," he said bleakly as the tall, skinny man on the boulder and the shorter one with the big rifle ambled toward him.

A new voice intruded. Into view stepped a beefy specimen in greasy buckskins who wore enough hardware to sink a boat. The man had a bushy brown beard and bushy brows which hid half his face. His laugh was like the sound made by a saw on a log. "What the hell is it with these city boys, Clell? They sure do call on the Almighty a powerful lot."

The scarecrow stepped to the edge of the boulder and propped his skinny hands on his equally skinny hips. "They ain't got no respect, little brother. They

17

figure that since they can't make do, the Almighty should bail 'em out every time they get in over their heads."

"Downright pitiful," declared the beefy specimen. He jabbed a thick thumb at Earl Fetterman. "What do you want me to do with this one? All he's doin' is sittin' there and quakin' like a leaf. It wouldn't hardly be sportin' to knock a puny sissy like him over the head."

Earl knew that he was being insulted again but this time he didn't care. He kept thinking that if he sat there and did nothing, maybe they would just go away and leave him alone.

The man named Clell sighed. "If he's that bad, let Razor do the chore. We don't give that critter enough to do for him to earn his keep as it is."

Pvt. Fetterman felt his insides freeze solid. The word RAZOR reverberated in his head like the peal of a bell during a funeral procession. He barely heard the beefy man shout the name, but he did see the massive gray streak of rippling sinews which flowed over the ground toward him. He saw the hairy form spring, saw its enormous mouth spring wide. Earl even saw wicked rows of gleaming, serrated teeth just before steely jaws clamped on his throat, and he knew that the creature had been aptly named.

Then someone was screaming and blubbering, forever and ever.

Chapter Two

The most wanted man in all of Arizona had not moved a muscle in over an hour.

From a low ridge which overlooked the ranch house belonging to the man Clay Taggart hated more than any other, he patiently spied on his avowed enemy.

If anyone had happened by and spotted Taggart on that ridge, they would have sworn he was an Apache. With good reason. Taggart's black hair was as long as an Apache's and held in place around his brow by a dusty white headband. He wore a breech-cloth, as would an Apache, and knee-high moccasins, the style favored by that tribe. His skin had been bronzed dark by the sun, as dark as that of the Apaches themselves. To complete the picture he presented, on his left hip he wore a Bowie, on his right a nickel-plated Colt, while slung over his chest was a bandoleer crammed with cartridges for the

Winchester cradled in his left elbow.

From a distance, Clay Taggart appeared every inch an Indian.

Anyone who saw him up close, though, would immediately know the truth. For up close they would see that Taggart's eyes were a clear lake-blue, unlike those of any Apache who ever lived. Up close they would also see that his features were sharper than those of most Apaches, that his nose was not as wide, his cheeks were not as broad, his forehead not quite as high. These were small differences, to be sure, but they were enough to conclusively prove that Clay Taggart was not an Indian.

And yet, sometimes physical features do not tell the whole story. Sometimes, features lie. A person's true nature is always buried deep within them, not on the surface of their skin.

So it was with Clay Taggart, the White Apache. In his mind and in his heart he viewed himself as a Chiricahua, as a brother to the renegades who had saved his life and befriended him. To Clay Taggart's way of thinking, he was every inch an Apache. He had thrown in his lot with them and he would live and die as they lived and died.

Nothing anyone could say or do would ever convince Taggart otherwise. He was a new man. He had been reborn the day a lynch party left him dangling at the end of a rope and Delgadito the renegade had him cut down before the noose had strangled the life from him.

In keeping with his new life, Taggart had a new name. It had been given to him by Delgadito. Lick-oyee-shis-inday, the Apaches called him. It meant White-Man-Of-The-Woods, and stemmed from the fact that the Apache name for their own tribe was Shis-Inday, or Men-Of-The-Woods. Few knew this.

Few were aware that 'Apache' was the name another tribe had given them.

It fit, though. For in the language of the other tribe, 'Apache' meant enemy, and the Shis-Inday regarded anyone not of their tribe as exactly that. It had always been so. It always would.

The Apache creed was simple, and taught to every boy before he was big enough to bend his first bow. Apache warriors must be masters at killing without being killed, and at stealing without being caught.

Delgadito and the other members of the renegade band had taught Clay Taggart much. He could now survive off the land just as they did. He could go for days with little water and less food. When he had to, he could blend into the background so as to be invisible. He could stalk quarry as silently as a mountain lion, strike as swiftly as a scorpion.

These were all skills Clay intended to fully use. Burning in his breast was a rage so fiery, a hatred so strong, that when he thought of it, his body would shake as if he were having a fit and his face would flush the color of blood.

Clay Taggart craved revenge on those who had wronged him. He lived, breathed and ate revenge. It was always at the back of his mind, even when he did other things, even when he appeared to concentrate on something else. Revenge! Sweet, vicious revenge against those who had lynched him and the man who had put them up to it, Miles Gillett.

Thanks to Gillett, Clay Taggart was now an outlaw. No, worse than an outlaw. He had been branded a traitor by the Army and the law alike. Every white person in the Territory was out for his blood. He'd be gunned down on sight, no questions asked.

The White Apache, they called him. Turncoat. Butcher. The vilest man who ever wore britches. If captured, he would be duly tried and then duly executed, either by firing squad if the U.S. Army got its hands on him or by having his neck stretched if the marshal of Tucson did the job.

Let them try! Taggart thought to himself as he peered at the cluster of buildings a quarter of a mile below. They would not take him alive. Of that he was sure. With his dying breath he would fight for his freedom. With his last ounce of strength he would resist those who had unjustly made an outcast of him.

Movement down at the ranch drew the White Apache's interest. A pair of figures had emerged from the grand house and were crossing to the stable and corral. The distance was too great for him to see their faces. But he did not need to see them to know that the mammoth slab of a man was Miles Gillett and the shapely woman with dark hair was Gillett's wife, Lilly.

The richest man in Arizona walked to the corral. The woman Clay had once loved more than life itself walked at Gillett's side, her slender arm linked in his huge one.

The White Apache quivered as if cold even though the blazing sun blistered the ground around him. It had been weeks since he last saw Lilly. Being this close, being reminded of the love they had once shared, was almost more than he could bear. And when he recollected how she had spurned him for Gillett, it set his innards to aching something terrible.

In the corral, the object of the Gilletts' interest

had lifted its gigantic head to stare at the pair. It lumbered a few steps nearer and tossed its head but did not try to attack as a longhorn would have done.

The story had proven to be true. When Clay first heard it, a day and a half ago, he'd had no way of knowing if it were fact or fiction. Folks, after all, did love to gossip, and half the time they didn't get their gossip straight.

At the time, Clay had been buried under several inches of loose dirt less than ten strides from a small spring. It was a favorite stop along the Tucson-Mesilla road. Practically everyone rested there, either coming or going. By secreting himself nearby, he often overheard information he could use.

That particular afternoon an old wagon had creaked up to the spring and two muleskinners had hopped down to water their team. They were savvy, those two; one kept watch with a cocked Henry while the other did the work. At first they had jabbered on about trifles; the hot weather, the pay they would receive for hauling their load of freight, and the latest rumors of Indian trouble. Then Clay's ears had perked up.

"Hey, did you hear tell about that uppity son of a bitch, Gillett?" asked the bearded hulk tending the mules.

The man holding the rifle had not acted very interested. "Who?"

"That rich rancher over to Tucson way. You remember, Ben. We hauled for him a few times. Once it was those fancy china dishes for his cow bunny. He about had a fit when she opened a crate and found one of the saucers had a tiny little crack. He took it out of our pay."

Ben had frowned. "Oh. Him. The bastard who

thinks he's the Almighty's gift to the rest of us. Yeah, I remember that curly wolf, Zeke. So what?"

"So the word is that he's gone and bought himself a big old bull from Texas to improve his herd."

Ben had stifled a yawn. "If you've seen one bull, you've seem 'em all."

"Oh?" Zeke had snickered. "Ever seen one worth twenty-thousand dollars before?"

The other muleskinner had tried to swallow his navel with his lower jaw. "You're joshin'. There ain't a critter been born worth that amount of money. Why, it's five times as much as most people make in a whole year!"

"Be that as it may," Zeke had said, "I have it straight from a gent who was there when they brung the animal into Tucson. He said that Gillett was goin' on and on about how much it cost, struttin' around like he always does."

"The damned rooster."

"Yep. Anyway, the story is that Gillett bought it from a jasper over to El Paso way who bought it from some high muck-a-muck over to Europe, or some such. Gillett figures to breed him a passel of cows, and every one will be worth its weight in gold."

Ben shook his head in disgust. "Strange, ain't it? How them that have a lot keep on gettin' more while we that don't have much wind up with less and less. Sort of makes a body suspect they plan it that way."

"Aw, you cantankerous old coot. You're just jealous because Miles Gillett is better lookin' than you are."

"If I had his money, I could look pretty too."

It had been hard for Clay Taggart to stay put for the 20 minutes the muleskinners took to finish and mosey on. Rising up out of the shallow depression, he had quickly filled it back in and jogged westward. He'd had to find out for himself.

And now Clay knew the story was true. He shifted to relieve a slight cramp in his left leg, then squinted up at the sun to gauge how long it would be until nightfall. Too long, unfortunately. It was still shy of noon.

But the White Apache was not about to leave. He was not about to pass up any chance to make Gillett pay for the nightmare ordeal he had been through.

Once, Clay had wanted to kill Gillett outright. Many an hour he had idled away dreaming of throttling Gillett with his bare hands or of pumping slug after slug into the rancher's twitching body.

Then one day it had occurred to Clay that killing Gillett outright was the wrong revenge to take. It was too easy on Gillett. The man would die and that would be the end of it. Gillett might experience a few fleeting moments of fear and some pain, but nowhere near enough to suit Clay.

Gillett had to feel the raw agony Clay had felt when the noose tightened on his throat. Gillett had to experience the supreme torment Clay had felt when he learned that the woman he adored had given herself to the man who had stolen his ranch out from under him.

Miles Gillett had to suffer as Clay had suffered, only worse. Much, much worse. Clay wanted Gillett to suffer as no human being had ever suffered in the entire history of the world.

To that end, Clay was going to chip away at the wealthy rancher. He was going to whittle Gillett down to the size of the slug Gillett resembled. Then, and only then, would he kill the man bit by bit by bit.

The notion brought a rare smile to Clay's weathered face. He was so caught up by the idea that for all of 30 seconds he daydreamed instead of staying fully alert as he should have. And so it was that he did not hear the clomp of approaching horses until they were almost on him.

The White Apache had picked his hiding place well. He lay on his belly among a half-dozen boulders only four yards below the rim. No one at the ranch could see him, unless through a spyglass.

But punchers drifting toward the bunkhouse were another matter. Twisting his head just enough to see the riders, White Apache stiffened. Four cowboys had crested the rise. The foremost was only ten feet away. All four wore six-shooters and carried rifles in saddle scabbards.

The White Apache knew that if he so much as sneezed, they would hear and tear into him with a vengeance. All of Gillett's hands were notorious for being loyal to the brand.

Watching out of the corner of his eye, Taggart was dismayed to see the leader rein up and the rest follow suit. The first puncher hooked a leg around his saddle horn, pulled out the makings, and set to rolling a smoke.

"Do we have time for this?" asked a stocky cowboy.

"It doesn't take all that long to light a cigarette," replied the man with the makings. He had a slow drawl which hinted at a Southern upbringing.

"Tell that to the boss, Vasco. He doesn't take kindly to shirkers. If you'd been with the Triangle G as long as the rest of us, you'd know better than to push your luck by bucking him. Miles Gillett is not an hombre to take lightly."

The man called Vasco chuckled. He was lanky

and limber and had the air of a hawk about him. "I never take anyone lightly, Williams. But after working hard all morning, I figure I deserve a smoke. If our boss holds it against me, all he has to do is give the word and I'll light a shuck. It makes no difference to me."

Williams bristled. "That's your problem right there, mister. You don't give a damn about anything or anyone except yourself. I saw that about you right away."

Vasco casually shifted, lowered his right hand to his waist, and hooked his thumb in his belt. His hand was now inches from a pearl-handled Colt worn butt forward on his left hip for a cross draw. When he spoke, the twang in his voice was replaced by an edge as hard as granite. "If I didn't know better, friend, I'd swear you just insulted me."

The White Apache saw the other men tense up. Williams made it a point not to move his arms and mustered a fake smile.

"I'm not loco, Vasco. I was just making a point, is all. Most of us who work for Mr. Gillett think he's the greatest ramrod this side of the Divide. We'd shine his boots if he asked. So naturally we'd never do anything that he wouldn't approve of."

Vasco nodded but kept his hand where it was. "That's the difference between you and me, Williams. I shine no man's boots. Ever." He finished making his cigarette and rolled it between his lips as if savoring the feel. Producing a match, he lit the tip with a flourish, then flicked the match aside. It sailed in a wide arc and hit a boulder near Clay Taggart.

The other three cowboys sat there as Vasco lifted his reins and trotted down the ridge. If looks could kill, he would have been a dead man long before he reached the bottom.

Williams cursed softly. "That cat-eyed leather slapper! I don't know where he gets off acting so high and mighty around the rest of us."

"His fancy lead chucker gives him the right," commented another. "A man with his rep can do as he damn well pleases. They say he's gunned down seven men so far."

This did not sit well with Williams, who cursed more and added, "I don't see why the boss keeps hiring no-accounts like him. There are more than enough hands to get the work done around here."

The second man took off his Stetson to wipe his perspiring brow. "It's not the cattle that Mr. Gillett was thinking of when he signed Vasco on. You know that as well as we do."

Again Williams swore. "Santee. Vasquez. Bonner. Now Vasco. We have more gun sharks working for us than most outlaw gangs do."

"Outlaws don't have to fret about Apaches," said the second man.

The third cowboy finally spoke. "Apaches, hell. The boss hired Vasco because of Taggart. Gillett still thinks that this so-called White Apache is going to come after him. It has him spooked."

Williams shook his head. "You're wrong, Carter. The boss isn't scared of any man. Why, he could beat the tar out of Clay Taggart without half working up a sweat. I know. I saw them together a few times before Taggart turned Ijnun."

Carter held his ground. "And I know what Vasquez told me. Since he's foreman, he should know."

"What did the greaser tell you?" Williams demanded.

"Only that Gillett hasn't been sleeping well for a

long time. He goes to bed with a loaded pistol under his pillow, and every little noise wakes him up. He's about driven his missus up the wall. She wants him to take a long vacation back East but Gillett won't go, not until this White Apache is good and buried."

Williams was a hard man to convince. "I won't believe that until I hear it from the boss's own lips. I've known Miles Gillett too long. The man doesn't know the meaning of fear." He touched his spurs to his horse, and all three of them rode on down the slope toward the stable.

Clay Taggart was having a run of luck. This made twice he had been in the right place at the right time. As he watched the cowboys depart, he mulled over what he had learned. It came as no surprise that Gillett had hired another gunman; the man had enough money to hire an army if he wanted. What did surprise Clay was finding out that he had Gillett spooked.

In a certain respect Clay was like Williams. As much as he despised Gillett, as much as he hated the man's devious, wicked nature, he would be the first to admit that Miles Gillett did not have a yellow bone in his body. He could not see Gillett being afraid of anyone.

Still, it was something to think on. It was something to ponder, Apache fashion.

Which Clay Taggart did, the rest of that morning and through the long, hot afternoon. He was a credit to his Chiricahua teachers. The heat had no effect. The lack of water did not phase him. Seldom did he so much as twitch. To a casual observer he would have appeared to be part and parcel of the boulders around him.

Evening came. At last welcome relief arrived in the form of a cool northwesterly breeze. Still, the

White Apache did not move from concealment. He stayed among the boulders while twilight faded and the sky darkened to the hue of indigo ink. Stars sparkled. A few at first, but more and more as time went by so that at length the heavens were filled with a myriad of twinkling pinpoints.

Even so, the White Apache made no attempt to rise.

Early on, lights appeared in the main house and the bunkhouse. Shadows flitted across windows. From the main house tinkled the music of a piano and the voice of a woman raised in song. From the bunkhouse rose the gruff voices of men arguing, playing cards and telling tall tales.

In time, the music ended. The voices faded. One by one the lights blinked out until the only source of light on the whole ranch was the lamp framed in a second story window of the ranch house. It, too, eventually blinked off, leaving a black emptiness where some semblance of life had been.

At last the White Apache stood. He stretched and rubbed limbs long unused to restore his circulation. Picking up his Winchester, he padded down the ridge with all the stealth of a stalking coyote.

As Clay Taggart neared the stable he dropped into a crouch and paused every few strides to look and listen. He did not think Gillett would bother to post guards all night, every night, but he could not take anything for granted. And while there had been no evidence of dogs, many ranchers had taken to keeping one or two around to keep watch. Gillett might have done the same.

When White Apache was close enough to the corral to see the enormous creature within, he eased onto his stomach and crawled. The bull appeared to be dozing on its feet. As yet it had not caught his scent. He worked his way to a water trough not far from the gate. There, he rose onto his knees.

The ranch was tranquil. No sounds came from either the main house or the bunkhouse. Nor was there any trace of anyone out for a late stroll.

The White Apache crept to the stable doors. They were closed but not barred. Easing one open just wide enough for him to slip inside, he quietly glided down the central aisle past stalls of sleeping horses and a few steers. Several of the animals snorted or fidgeted but none raised an outcry.

At the back of the stable, under the loft, bales of hay had been stacked. Gripping one, White Apache threw it over his left shoulder, steadied himself, and hurried back outside.

The bull grunted and raised its ponderous head as White Apache stepped to the rails and slowly lowered the bale to the ground. Then, after leaning the Winchester against a post, he sank flat and snaked under the bottom rail. The bale hid him from the bull. He heard the animal sniff as he drew the Bowie to quickly cut the twine.

The sweet grass spilled out into a pile. White Apache did the same with the hay as he had done with the dirt that time at the spring. He sprinkled it over his body, covering himself as best he was able in the short time he had before the bull gave a rumble deep in its barrel chest and started toward him from the far end of the corral.

White Apache clutched the Bowie firmly in his right hand. He glued his eyes to the animal, marking its every step, taking its measure and being impressed by what he saw.

Clay Taggart had been a rancher not all that long ago. He knew how to pick quality horseflesh and cattle. The bull coming toward him was a breed

31

new to him, but its size and shape and the way it moved, its total symmetry, clearly showed the generations of breeding which had gone into producing so magnificent a brute.

It stood over seven feet high at the shoulders and was as broad as a buffalo. Its horns were short in comparison to a longhorn's, but there was no doubt that a single toss of that corded neck would disembowel man or beast.

Clay Taggart, the rancher, was awed. White Apache, the renegade, had no time for such sentiments. For as much as he might admire the animal, it made no difference. It would not stop him from doing what had to be done. He had come there for one reason and one reason alone.

To kill it.

Chapter Three

It would have been child's play for Clay Taggart to have picked off the bull from a distance with the Winchester. A single shot through the skull from a hundred yards out would have done the job nicely. It would also have given Clay plenty of time to slip away before the cowboys spilled from the bunkhouse and fanned out to find him.

By rights, that is what Clay should have done. It was quicker. It was safer. It was the smart thing to do. But, as with slaying Gillett outright, it would have been too easy. And it would also rob him of the deep feeling of satisfaction he would get from doing it the way he had planned.

As the bull lumbered toward him, White Apache coiled his steely arms and legs. The creature sniffed loudly again and again. White Apache could only hope that the delicious aroma of the hay would smother his own scent or so overpower it that the bull would not realize its mistake until too late.

The animal's hide was dark brown, which made its features hard to see in the dark. It halted a few steps away and bent its giant head from side to side, as if studying the pile. Warm, fetid breath gushed from its lungs, stirring the hay and washing over the prone man. A huge hoof pawed the ground.

For tense moments the bull simply stood there. It could not seem to make up its mind whether to take a bite or not.

White Apache scarcely breathed. The towering mountain of muscle edged nearer and lowered its mouth to nip at the edge of the hay. Its large teeth crunched loudly. It swallowed, snorted, and took one more step. Now its head was right above White Apache. Looking up, he saw the underside of its wide chin and the many loose folds of flesh which were his target.

White Apache coiled his legs, then exploded upward, wrapping his left arm around the bull's neck even as he buried the Bowie in the creature's neck, not once but several times. The bull uttered a grunt of surprise and started to back up. White Apache plunged the blade in once more, twisted it, and slashed from right to left, severing hide and blood vessels from one side of its throat to the other. A sticky, warm geyser spouted downward over his shoulders and chest. In the blink of an eye White Apache was drenched.

Bulls were not the brightest of animals. It took a few more seconds for this one to register the fact that it was being attacked, and to react. Suddenly throwing itself into the air, it whirled as it came down and shook itself as a dog might to shake off an unwanted flea. When that failed to work, it bucked like a bronco.

White Apache clung on for dear life. He stabbed and stabbed, slicing the neck to ribbons, while more and more blood cascaded over him. The monster's front hooves slammed down so close to his body that flying bits of dirt peppered his face and torso. Over and over he was yanked high into the air, then flung at the ground so hard that his teeth jarred together. His legs and hips were battered mercilessly.

The bull abruptly stopped. It planted its legs wide and commenced whipping its body from side to side while at the same time it forked its sharp horns down at its tormentor.

White Apache held on with both arms and tucked his knees to his chest. He was snapped from side to side so violently that his arms were nearly torn from their sockets. His body smacked the earth repeatedly. Pain lanced him without let up. He began to think that he had let his thirst for vengeance blind his judgment, that it would have been better to kill the brute from a distance than to attempt the feat with his own two hands.

Unexpectedly, the bull straightened and ran toward the fence. Head down, hooves flying, it pounded to within a few feet of the rails before it veered aside and circled the corral at breakneck speed. Its movements grew more frantic with every passing moment.

Less blood poured onto White Apache. His arms were already so slick, though, that he had trouble holding on. When the bull cut to the right, he felt his hands start to go. Rather than make a futile effort to regain his purchase, he let himself be hurled loose and rolled with the momentum. Like a spinning top he shot over a dozen feet before he came to rest on his left side, facing Gillett's pride and joy.

The bull was staring right at him. It pawed the earth, bobbed its head, and charged.

White Apache knew what those flailing hooves would do to his body. The bull was already so close that he had no time to leap to his feet and flee. All he could do was throw himself to one side and roll like a madman. He heard the bull go pounding by, and the instant it passed, he sprang erect.

For such a massive brute, the bull was amazingly quick and agile. It whirled in a twinkling and came after him, head down, horns cocked to gore.

The fence seemed miles off. White Apache flew toward it, his arms and legs pumping. He did not look back. He did not need to. The bull's breath was warm on his back and he swore that the ground under him trembled as if to an earthquake. There was thunder in his ears, but whether it was the wild hammering of his own heart or the hammering of the creature's hooves he honestly couldn't say.

Suddenly the rails were right there in front of him. White Apache hurled himself into the air. His left hand caught hold of the top one and he catapulted himself up and over. He was going so fast that he was unable to keep from tumbling when something hit his hip a jolting blow. For harrowing moments he sailed head over heels, to land on his shoulder with enough force to knock the breath from his lungs and leave him gasping and helpless, at the bull's mercy.

As if through a gray haze, White Apache could hear the animal snort and stomp. Mustering his strength, he turned his head.

The bull was still inside, its dripping muzzle pressed between two of the rails, its dark eyes fixed on him in hellish hatred. It could have smashed through with ease, reducing the timbers to so much kindling, and been on him in a flash. But habit won out over hatred.

White Apache fought to clear his head as he propped his hands under him and struggled to stand. He had the presence of mind to glance at the bunkhouse and the main house. All was quiet. No lights had come on. No doors had opened. It would have been a different story if the bull had smashed out of the corral. And Gillett's men still might be roused from slumber if the animal made a lot of noise in its death throes.

Hefting the Bowie, White Apache walked around the corral to the far side. As he wanted, the bull shadowed him, glaring all the while. He stopped near the Winchester. Now all he had to do was wait.

The bull stood a few feet away, wheezing like a bellows. Every so often it would give a mighty shake of its head. It swayed from time to time but always recovered.

White Apache did not clean off his knife. Not yet, anyway. He simply watched as the animal slowly weakened. Many minutes went by, but he did not move.

As a tribute to the bull's stamina, almost an hour elapsed before it swayed for perhaps the fortieth time. This time, however, it lost its balance and fell heavily, straight down. It tried to get back up, its legs thrashing wildly. But it could not.

Another twenty minutes were gone when the animal finally snorted and rolled onto its side. For the longest while it breathed softly, its tail twitching every now and then. At long, long last it exhaled loudly and was still.

White Apache wasted no more time. A lithe bound took him over the corral fence. He alighted close to the bull, poised to flee in case it revived.

His concern on that score proved groundless. It was indeed dead.

Bending over the neck, White Apache set to work. The Bowie was sharp but the hide was tough and the flesh thick with muscle. He broke out in a sweat as he sawed clean down to the bone. It proved difficult to turn the head when he needed to go further until he set down the knife, spread his legs wide, gripped a horn in each hand, and twisted.

For the most part, White Apache worked in silence. The night wind carried the occasional yip of coyotes. At times one of the animals in the stable would make a noise, but never loud enough to be heard up at the house or by the cowhands.

In due course White Apache had the neck severed, but his work was not quite done. He went to the trough, washed the Bowie clean, and dried it on his loincloth. After sliding the blade into its beaded sheath, he returned to the bull. The head now lay bent at a strange angle. The tongue jutted from parted lips. Again he gripped the horns and braced himself.

Shoulders bunching, White Apache gave the head a violent wrench. It twisted, but not sharply enough to do what had to be done. Once more he tried, with a similar result. Taking a few deep breaths and firming his arms, he jerked his body around, throwing his entire weight into the movement. The head lifted, bent. He heaved, straining. The snap of the neck bone breaking was like the crack of a derringer.

White Apache nearly fell on his face when the head gave way under him. He dug in his heels, rose, and faced the buildings. No one appeared, and he was turning back to the task at hand when a latch rasped faintly and the door to the bunkhouse swung inward.

Instantly White Apache dashed to the rails. He was up and over quicker than a lizard could have done. Reclaiming the Winchester, he sprinted around the stable to the far corner. From there he could see that a single puncher had emerged and was hurrying over.

The man was an older hand, sporting a grizzled chin and hair cropped short. He had on an undershirt with holes in it and his pants. In his right hand he held a rifle. As he neared the stable he worked the lever and slowed down.

Clay Taggart reined in an impulse to curse a blue streak. He did not need this, not when he was so close. Staying well hid until the front of the stable blocked the cowboy from sight, he sprinted forward, careful not to step on anything that might give him away. At the front corner, White Apache stopped.

The hand was 30 feet away, close to the corral but not quite close enough to see the bull clearly. The man was looking every which way and acted puzzled. No doubt he had heard the neck break but he could not figure out what had made the noise. Slowly turning, he moved nearer to the rails.

It would be all over once the puncher saw the bull. The man would shout to high heaven and the rest of the cowboys would rush out to see what all the fuss was about.

White Apache thought fast. Spinning on a heel, he raced back around to the rear of the stable. The back door was closed but opened readily. He ran up the aisle to a stall containing a cow. Opening it, he grabbed the startled animal by the ear and steered it toward the front. The wide double doors were still ajar, so all he had to do was give the cow a swat on the rump and it walked on out as if taking a moonlit stroll.

"Bessy? What the hell are you doing loose? Did that damned Johnson forget to pen you in again? He knows how you like to wander."

White Apache darted into the shadows. Through a crack he saw the old cowboy take hold of the cow and lead her back.

"I've got to have another talk with that yack. You're our best milker, and I can't have you traipsing off every time you get it into your head that you need to gallivant." The man rubbed her neck affectionately. "Without your milk, girl, the vittels I ship up would be a sight less tasty."

The man was the cook. As any rancher knew, the cookie was the heart and soul of every cow outfit. He not only kept the hands fed and a hot pot of coffee ready at any hour of the day, he acted as nursemaid when punchers were busted up, watched over bedrolls when a drive was under way, acted as banker when men had loose change which needed to be kept safe, and always had a ready ear for any problem or complaint which might arise.

Clay had many fond memories of the cooks he had known. So now, as the grizzled man pushed on the door to usher Bessy back into the stable, a mental tug of war took place. Part of Clay wanted to spare him. Another part of him wanted to bury the Bowie to the hilt. He put his hand on the knife but wavered, torn by the two conflicting urges.

Bessy ambled inside and on down the aisle. The cook strode only a few steps behind her, grinning.

From out of the darkness swooped Clay Taggart. His arms swept up. The cookie caught the motion out of the corner of his eye and pivoted, bringing his own rifle to bear. Clay struck first, smashing the stock of the Winchester into the cook's temple. A second blow was not needed. The cook dropped in his tracks like a poled ox.

White Apache stepped back and regarded the unconscious man a moment. It was fortunate, he mused, that none of the other members of the band had been there. Fiero, especially, would mock him for being so weak. An Apache never spared an enemy when there was no need.

Bessy had stopped to look around in dull confusion. Clay gave her a healthy swat on the backside and she took off toward her stall as if her tail were on fire. He moved to the double doors. A quick check verified no one else had appeared so he dashed to the corral and scaled the rails.

The bull's head was heavy. Instead of lifting it, Clay took hold of a horn with one hand so his other hand would be free to use a gun, and dragged the grisly trophy to the gate. Once he had the gate open, he continued dragging the head out of the corral and on across the neatly tended yard which separated the stable from the house.

The head left a gory smear in its wake. Clay deliberately dragged it through a flower garden and then up a tidy walk to the front porch. To his right sat a bench flanked by a trellis. To his left, a settle draped with flowery vines the likes of which he had never seen before. They were as much out of place in Arizona as swamp grass would be. He knew that Lilly must have had the plants sent from somewhere back in the States, which made them precious to her. Out of sheer spite he went over and cut every last vine to shreds.

Most men would have been satisfied at that point. They would have left the bull's head on the bench or the settle or in front of the door. But not Clay Taggart. He wanted to strike the fear of God into Miles Gillett, and to do that, he had to take a gamble most men would label insane.

Clay tried the screen door. It was unlocked. Nor was the inner door barred. Which was not at all unusual out in the country, where folks tended to trust one another—and in Providence. Doors were rarely locked. In fact, the man who took up the practice was often viewed with suspicion. What was wrong with him, the common sentiment went, that he saw fit to shut out his own neighbors?

The Winchester, Clay left propped against the jamb. He braced the screen door wide with a foot, then hauled the head inside and set it on the polished floorboards in the hall. Grinning in sadistic glee, he dragged it past several rooms to the foot of a staircase.

The house was as still as a tomb. It was so quiet that Clay could hear the raspy growl of someone sawing logs upstairs. Gripping both horns, he toted his prize to the landing and there paused to get his bearings.

There were two doors on the right, one on the left. Clay crept to the latter and peeked within. When he set eyes on the pair in the canopy bed, he gave a start, even though he expected them to be there. His pulse quickened and the room seemed to spin before him, so intense were his emotions. It took every ounce of self-control he had to keep him from drawing his six-shooter and finishing the pair off then and there.

Asleep in the bed were Miles and Lilly Gillett. The rancher was on his wide back, a forearm draped over his brow. Lilly lay curled on her right side, her lower lip fluttering as she breathed.

Clay's memory was jolted by her beauty. Inwardly he traveled back to the days before his life fell apart, to the time before Lilly had been forced to wed Gillett to save her father's ranch, to the days when the two of them were together all the time and talking seriously of marriage and the family they would have.

A thrill tingled Clay's spine. It was as if he had stripped off the years, and there he was, running hand-in-hand across a sunny meadow with Lilly at his side. Her long hair flew in the wind as she laughed in gay abandon and turned eyes filled with love on him. They halted under the limbs of a willow on the bank of a gleaming river and kissed as they had kissed hundreds of time before. The lush feel of her ripe body, her warmth, the musky scent of her perfume, all combined to make Clay's head swim.

Lilly had always had that effect on him. She had been the one great love of his life and she had thrown that love up in his face. There were times when merely thinking about it was enough to make Clay want to scream.

This was one of those times. Clay clenched his fists and grit his teeth and allowed the feeling to pass before he went on about the chore he had set for himself.

Miles Gillett appeared to be out to the world. Which struck Clay as odd, given the comments he had overheard on the ridge. The cowboy named Carter had claimed that Gillett was having trouble sleeping nights, and waking up at the drop of a feather. Yet there the man snored.

Then Clay spotted the bottle on the nightstand beside the bed. His moccasins made no noise on the plush rug as he walked over and lifted it to the

43

window. The scrawl was hard to read but he recognized it as the handwriting of old Doc Sawyer in Tucson. The sawbones had prescribed the concoction for stomach trouble and bad nerves.

So.

The stories were true.

White Apache's eyes lit with sadistic glee as he stealthily went back around to the hallway and brought the head inside. He froze when Lilly shifted and muttered under her breath. She smacked her red lips a few times, curled up on her other side, and was sleeping peacefully in moments.

The sheet had slid partially off her. Clay saw her full figure from the waist up. He saw how her bosom strained against her sheer nightgown and the rise and fall of her flat belly as she breathed, and a lump formed in his throat. Swallowing, he went to the landing for the bull's head and brought it to the foot of the bed.

Now came the truly difficult part. Even people who were hard to wake up would do so instantly if they felt someone—or something—crawl into bed with them.

Clay Taggart slowly lowered the head to the quilt. He had to shove both hands up under the folds of the neck to keep it from slipping. Exercising the utmost care, he eased the head down so that the back of it rested on the footboard. The bed barely sagged.

Miles Gillett abruptly stirred. His arm dropped to his side and he rolled to the left. His eyes seemed to blink once or twice. For a few moments it appeared that he was about to wake up. But once he had rolled over, he subsided, his chin drooping to his chest. He snored louder than ever.

Trackers

Ever so slowly, Clay slid his fingers out from under the neck. They were caked with flecks of blood and gore. He looked around. The pink canopy caught his eye. Reaching up, he wiped his hands on the ruffle.

Clay backed from the bedroom. He paused in the doorway, once again torn by two desires. On the one hand, he yearned to go over to Gillett and slit the bastard from ear to ear. On the other, he wanted to torment his enemy Apache-style, to make Gillett endure living hell before he finally evened the score.

It was Lilly who decided the issue. She rolled onto her back at that exact moment. The sheet shifted lower still, exposing her exquisite figure down to the knees. Pale starlight bathed her, imbuing her with such stark beauty that it took Clay Taggart's breath away. It also reminded him of how much he had lost, of how much Miles Gillett had to atone for.

No, Clay decided. Killing the man would have to wait. There would be another time, another place. As soundless as a specter, he glided to the landing and down to the first floor. The wind whipped his long hair as he stepped onto the porch and retrieved the Winchester.

White Apache was halfway along the gravel walk when he spied a figure near the stable. The cook had revived much sooner than he had expected and was crawling toward the bunkhouse. Swiftly, White Apache ran over.

The man was so weak that he could hardly lift an arm. Blood trickled from a nasty gash in his temple, down over his cheek and chin. His head was so low to the ground that he did not realize he was no longer alone until he extended his right hand and his fingers brushed White Apache's foot. Going rigid, the man glanced up. "Oh, God!" he croaked. "Not you!"

"Do you know who I am?" Clay asked quietly.

The sourdough managed to nod.

"How?"

"Your eyes."

Clay Taggart hunkered down. "There was a cook named Brewster once. He worked for my pa. He took a shine to me and used to make me son-of-a-bitch-in-a-sack every chance he could. If you ever run into him, tell him how obliged you are."

"For what?"

"For your life," Clay Taggart said, and slammed the stock against the man's jaw. The cook sagged. This time he would be out for quite a while.

Rising, Clay walked into the stable and selected the finest horse there, a roan stallion. It behaved itself as he led it out onto the plain, swung up bareback, and applied his heels. In moments the night closed around him, and he chuckled, quite pleased with himself.

Little did White Apache know that the last laugh was not to be his.

Chapter Four

Col. Thomas Reynolds rode around a bend in the Tuscon-Mesilla road. Ahead on a hill to the west reared the stone ramparts of Fort Bowie. The officer smiled. He looked forward to getting back to the post. First, he would treat himself to a glass of excellent brandy. Then he would have the orderly fill his tub with hot water so he could soak for an hour. It was the very least he deserved, he told himself, after putting up with the heat and the dust and the Chiricahuas.

Col. Reynolds glanced over his right shoulder at the detachment of Fifth Cavalry clattering up the road behind him. A week ago, when they had left the post, every man had been dressed in a clean, crisp uniform, and every saddle and bridle had practically shone. Now every trooper, every mount, was covered thick with dust. From head to toe, or from mane to tail, they were all a grimy grey.

But that was Arizona for you, Reynolds mused. In all his years he had never seen any country so foreboding. And it wasn't just the heat or the wind or the dust. It was the land itself, a land so harsh that even the creatures it bred and the vegetation it spawned were nightmares in their own right. Spiders the size of a man's hand. Snakes with fangs that dripped venom. Lizards that would bite down and never let go. Plants with spikes and barbs and thorns.

Small wonder, Reynolds noted, that the people who called this land home were as hard as the country in which they lived. Never had he met any tribe like the Apaches, and he had served on the Plains for years, dealing often with the Sioux and the Cheyenne and the Arapaho.

Without being obvious about it, Col. Reynolds shifted to glance at their Apache scout. Klo-sen was a Mescalero. His name, Reynolds had learned, meant 'Hair Rope,' and had something to do with the time he had strangled a Mexican soldado with a rope made of human hair.

Once Klo-sen had told Reynolds a little about his upbringing. How he had been trained to stay awake for an entire day without feeling the effects. How as a boy he had often been given water to carry in his mouth and told to run five miles or more without swallowing. How by the time he was a young man he could travel the equivalent of 70 miles in a single day, on foot, without tiring. How he had trained with knife and bow and lance and sling and rifle and war club until he could use them all with superior skill.

What astounded Reynolds the most was the fact that Klo-sen was not unique. To the contrary, the scout was typical of the men of his tribe. Quite average. Which made Reynolds all the more willing to believe the incredible tales of prowess he had heard about warriors who were more than average.

Such as Delgadito, the Chiricahua. The renegade had been a thorn in the Army's side since before Col. Reynolds arrived in the Territory. Striking at will, escaping without a trace, these were Delgadito's hallmarks. It was rightfully claimed that he had slain more Americans and Mexicans than any Apache alive.

And now, to make a bad situation much worse, a white traitor had joined forces with the renegade. Together they were spreading terror from one end of Arizona to the other. Clay Taggart, the White Apache, had to be stopped at all costs. That was the order Reynolds had been given. In no uncertain terms it was made clear that if he did not bring the White Apache to bay soon, his career would suffer accordingly.

So, a week ago, Reynolds had gone to pay Palacio, the chief of the Chiricahuas, another visit. They had smoked and eaten. The wily chief had listened while Reynolds stressed the urgency of the crises. Palacio had promised to do all in his power to help. But Palacio had made promises before, and the White Apache and Delgadito were still at large.

Now Reynolds was on his way back. In his eyes the trip had been a complete waste. He would never have gone if not for the insistent urging of his superiors. Yet they would blame him when no results were forthcoming.

The thud of hooves brought an end to the officer's reverie. Capt. Gerald Forester, a tough veteran of the Apache campaign, came alongside and asked the question uppermost on Reynolds's mind. "So what now, sir?"

The colonel frowned. "I wish to hell I knew," he admitted.

Forester was one of the few subordinates whose judgment he trusted. The rest were either green boys fresh out of the academy or borderline derelicts who could not keep their nose out of a bottle. "I'm open to any ideas you might have."

Forester wished that he had one. He respected Reynolds, which was more than could be said of some of the superior officers he had served under, and he would like to help. He knew what was at stake. But the colonel had already tried everything there was to try and nothing had worked. The White Apache had more lives than a cat. "I'll think on it, sir," was all he could say.

The road wound up around the hill to the front gate. A sentry in the east guard tower had seen them approaching from a long way off. As a result, the gate was already open and soldiers were lined up on both sides, standing at attention, their carbines held at the Present Arms position.

At the head of the line stood Lt. James Petersen. All spit and polish, he was the newest arrival at Fort Bowie and eager to prove his worth. He gave a properly stiff salute as the detachment reined up. It took an effort for him to keep a grin off his face, so pleased was he with his own performance. He couldn't wait to share the news.

Col. Reynolds had always been an observant man. He could not help but notice that the corners of the young lieutenant's mouth quirked upward several times as he wearily dismounted. Removing a gauntlet, he brushed dust from his sleeve, returned the salute, and said, "At ease, Petersen. I trust all went well while I was gone?"

"Not exactly, sir."

Worry stabbed deep into the colonel. He had left the junior officer in charge against his better judgment. There had been no choice. Of the four captains under his command, two had been out on patrol, one had been in Tucson on official business, and he'd had to take Forester with him to help interpret. "What do you mean, Lieutenant?"

Petersen reported in his best clipped voice, as he had been taught at the prestigious military academy he attended. "Deserters, sir. Three of them. Privates Earl Fetterman, James Koch, and William Stillwell did not show up for morning roll-call three days ago. I ordered an immediate search of the post. It was determined that three horses and provisions were missing."

Reynolds sighed. Desertion was a chronic problem at a number of forts in the Southwest, not just Bowie. The harsh climate, the unforgiving land, the Apaches and Comanches and other hostiles, all made military life a living hell. Some men simply could not take it. "Very well. I'll send Capt. Forester and Klo-sen after them."

Petersen beamed proudly. "That won't be necessary, sir. I've already dispatched trackers to hunt them down."

"Oh?" Col. Reynolds said, puzzled. His other scouts were all off in the Dragoons, so far as he knew. "Did Sieber and the others come back sooner than expected?"

"No, sir," Lt. Petersen said. "I sent the Bowdrie brothers."

Col. Reynolds thought his heart had stopped. For a few moments the world around him spun. He heard Capt. Forester curse and Sgt. McKinn's intake of breath. Steadying himself, he somehow was able to keep his voice calm as he said, "The Bowdrie

51

brothers are not on the military payroll, Lieutenant."

Petersen knew that something was amiss but he had no idea what. "The Army has hired them in the past. You told me so, yourself. And since they happened to be at the fort when the three troopers skipped, I thought it would be best to temporarily hire their services again." He paused. "You did tell me that they are three of the best trackers around, didn't you, sir?"

Capt. Forester wanted to throttle the junior officer. Turning away, he clenched both hands and said to no one in particular, "Dear God. It must already be too late."

"Sir?" Lt. Petersen said, glancing from the captain to the colonel. "Since no scouts were available and you were gone, I went by the book. Did I do wrong?"

Reynolds bowed his head. He couldn't blame the younger man for what had happened. A few weeks ago he had indeed mentioned that the Bowdrie brothers were good trackers, but only in passing. They had been talking about scouts in general, and how few white men could hold their own against the Indians. "I'm afraid you might have made a grievous mistake, yes."

Petersen felt the blood drain from his face. The last thing he wanted was to foul up so soon after arriving there. "May I ask how, sir?"

It was Capt. Forester who answered. Whirling, he said with great emotion, "The Bowdrie boys are killers, Petersen. Sure, they're about the best at what they do. Sure, they can track a lizard over hard ground. But they only do it for money. And they have a habit of killing whoever they're sent after." He paused to rein in his anger. "We've used them in the past, but only when no one else was handy. And we always made it a point to send troopers along with them to keep them in line. Did you send anyone this time?"

"No, sir," Petersen admitted. "But I did make it clear that they were to bring the three deserters back alive. I stressed that fact several times," he emphasized, hoping it would count in his favor. "They were not to harm the deserters unless the deserters resisted."

"We can always hope," Capt. Forester said forlornly.

Almost on cue, the sentry on the northwest guard tower let out with a bellow. "Duty Officer to the main gate! The Bowdries are coming in! With bodies."

Feeling as if his own body suddenly weighed a ton, Col. Reynolds turned and stepped to the left so he could see the riders. They were still well off, engulfed in a shimmering haze of heat. Strung out in single file, each buckskin clad figure led another horse over which a body had been draped. Behind the riders trailed a lupine form Reynolds was only too familiar with.

An awful silence had fallen over Fort Bowie. Every last soldier had stopped whatever he was doing to watch and wait. Many wore expressions of horror and loathing. Some betrayed fear, as if afraid the same fate might befall them one day. More showed resentment, and many of them fingered their carbines or pistols.

Lt. Petersen was aghast. "They can't have, sir!" he blurted. "I mean, I gave them very precise orders."

"Rank means nothing to vermin like the Bowdries," Capt. Forester commented. "And you did give them the perfect excuse."

"I did, sir?"

"You told them that they could fight back if the deserters resisted. The minute you said that, those poor boys were as good as dead, whether they resisted or not."

Presently the clomp of hooves heralded the arrival of the three trackers. If they noticed the cold reception, they did not show it. Swinging wide of the detachment, they made straight for the commanding officer.

Col. Reynolds clasped his hands behind his back and squared his shoulders. He would be damned if he would let them see how distraught he was. He would not give them that satisfaction. As they drew near, he tried to remember which one was which.

In the lead, on a mule, rode Clem Bowdrie. He favored a coonskin cap and an old Sharps buffalo gun. He also liked to wear the baggiest buckskins of any man alive. His blue eyes constantly flicked to the right and left and back again, never still for an instant. He was always as wary as a cornered cougar and three times as dangerous.

Next in line came Clell Bowdrie. The man had to be as skinny as a rail. He also had a reputation for being as tough as a grizzly. In addition to a Winchester and a Colt, he went around with a bow and quiver slung over his back. Rumor had it the bow was Cherokee-made. His brown hair hung to the middle of his back and had been fastened at shoulder height with a band of leather.

Last, also on a mule, entered Tick Bowdrie. The man was as rank as a festering sore. He liked to boast that he never, ever bathed, and anyone who came within breathing distance would not see fit to doubt him. Few, though, would have the gall to come right out and tell him that he smelled like a two-footed skunk. Not when he carried the arsenal he did.

Tick wore a pair of Remingtons wedged under his wide brown belt on either side of the big buckle. He had a Bowie on his right hip, a Colt on his left. Crisscrossing his chest were bandoleers, one for the Spencer he always carried, another for the shotgun slung across his back. Jutting from the top of his left boot was the hilt of an Arkansas toothpick. And word had made the rounds that he carried a derringer in the other boot. It was a standing joke that if Tick Bowdrie ever came unhorsed in deep water, he'd sink like a rock before he could draw a breath.

The last member of the killer clan had four paws and a shaggy coat that gave it the look of an unkempt bear. Only it wasn't a bear. Razor, as the beast was called, was part wolf and part something else. No one knew what the something else might be, but it was safe to say that whatever it had been had to have been as big as a bear and twice as mean.

Clem Bowdrie reined up before Colonel Reynolds. The tracker did not mince words. "We're here for our money. Fifty dollars each was what was agreed on. We'll take it in coin money, not that script stuff."

"Hello to you, too," Colonel Reynolds said testily. Stepping to the first corpse, he lifted the man's head by the hair. Despite himself, he recoiled. The mangled face was beyond recognition. "Dear God in heaven. What the hell did you do to him?"

Clem Bowdrie smiled, showing a row of small, white teeth. "Razor."

There was no need for the man to elaborate. Colonel Reynolds glanced at the beast, which squatted on its haunches a dozen feet away, its tongue lolling, its eyes like pinpoints of infernal fire as it met his gaze and held it. "I suppose all three of them resisted?" he asked icily.

"Sure as shootin'," Clem replied good-naturedly. "We did our best to take 'em alive, but your soldier boys was powerful determined not to be brought back."

Capt. Forester had gone over to examine the second body. He recognized Pvt. Koch. The huge exit wound between the shoulder blades told him which of the trackers was responsible. Only a Sharps could make a hole that big.

The truth was that Forester had not liked Trooper Koch very much. The New Yorker had done nothing but complain and shirk his duty from the day he arrived. But Koch had been a cavalryman, and Gerald Forester was cavalry through and through. He would gladly give his life for any man in his command. And he could not stand there and keep his mouth shut when one of their own had needlessly died. Before he could stop himself, he muttered, "You're a damned liar."

Tick Bowdrie was nearest. He flushed scarlet and snapped, "I heard that, mister. You'd best apologize or you'll regret the day you ever insulted a Bowdrie."

Forester took a step back, his right hand inches from his revolver. He knew the Tennessean could get off at least two shots before he cleared leather, but he didn't care. "Like hell I'll apologize. I don't think you tried to take them alive. I doubt you even gave them a chance to defend themselves."

Tick started to raise the Spencer. Nearby soldiers elevated their carbines. The threat of violence hung heavy in the hot air. And at that tense moment, when frayed nerves were about to snap, Clell Bowdrie laughed.

"Now don't this beat all! Here my kin and me do you boys in blue a favor, and look at what happens when we carry out our end of the arrangement?" Leaning toward Forester, he smiled, a smile as sinister as the look of a rattler right before it struck. "A man ought to be almighty careful of the words he throws around. If you'll take a good look at the three we brought back, you'll see that not a one was shot in the back."

"That's right," Clem threw in, indignant. "Say what you will about us Bowdries, there ain't a man among you who can accuse us of being no-account bushwhackers."

Col. Reynolds had no love for the Bowdries. In fact, he detested them. He would just as soon see their lifeless carcasses being fed on by buzzards as look at them. But he would be a poor excuse for an officer if he allowed blood to be spilled right there in the fort. Taking a stride, he plastered a grin on his face and held up both hands. "Now, now. That will be quite enough. No one is accusing you Bowdries of being bushwhackers. Lt. Petersen hired you to do a job, and you did it." He indicated the headquarters buildings. "If you will be so kind as to report to the adjutant's office, you will receive your money." Reynolds lowered his arms. "Then you will promptly leave this post and never set foot in it again so long as I am in command."

Clem shrugged. "That suits us right fine, Colonel. We should of knowed better than to take work for you blue-bellies. There ain't a one of you but don't have a tongue smeared with hog fat, and that's a born fact."

Col. Reynolds was not quite sure he understood the reference to hog fat. Just understanding the tracker's speech took some doing, since at times

Clem's high-pitched, Southern drawl was thick enough to be cut with a butter knife. And the others were little better. "Let's just chalk this whole affair up to a tragic mistake and let it go at that," he suggested.

"Whatever you say, Yankee." Clem let go of the lead rope and made for the headquarters, the Sharps tilted down so that it covered the troopers he passed. His brother fell into step behind him while the mongrel wolf brought up the rear.

Sgt. Joe McKinn waited until they were out of earshot to say, "Is it me, sir, or do they make your flesh crawl too?"

A majority of the soldiers present were staring at the three Southerners in ill-concealed hatred. Reynolds had to remind himself that the three slain troopers had friends. He would not put it past one of them to open fire. "Attention!" he thundered, and was pleased when they scrambled to obey.

"You heard the man, Private!" Capt. Forester bawled at a trooper who did not react fast enough. "When you're told to snap to, you damn well better!"

The colonel barked orders, dispersing the detachment and directing that the bodies be taken to the hospital for the time being. In the hustle and bustle of soldiers moving off in all directions, he didn't realize until another minute went by that Lt. Petersen was not there.

The junior officer had pivoted on a boot heel and stormed after the Bowdrie brothers. He was beside himself with fury that they had taken advantage of him and made him out to be incompetent in the eyes of his commanding officer and half the command. The trio were dismounting when he reached them. "I want a word with you," he announced.

Clem Bowdrie looked at him in amusement, which only fueled Petersen's anger.

"What can we do for you, soldier boy?" the Tennessean asked.

"It's what you didn't do that counts," the lieutenant responded. "I wanted those troopers brought back alive. I made that perfectly clear at the outset. Yet you saw fit to haul them back over a saddle."

Tick snickered. "We've just been all through this with the head of the pack. We don't hardly need to explain ourselves to no cub."

Clem laughed and went to turn away.

Something inside of James Petersen snapped. Without thinking, the officer grabbed the tracker's shoulder and spun the man around. Almost instantly the muzzle of the Sharps was jammed up under his jaw and the hammer clicked back. Tick and Clell also trained their rifles on him. And the wolf crouched, growling deep in its chest, ready to spring.

Lt. James Petersen froze. He was a blink of an eye away from dying, and he knew it.

"No man lays a hand on me, mister!" Clem Bowdrie rasped. "Not unless he's got my permission."

Tick Bowdrie moved in, his Spencer leveled. "I ought to put one into your gut for that, blue-belly, so you'll die nice and slow."

"No one touches Clem," Clell interjected fiercely. "No one. Not ever."

Petersen's mouth was so dry that he could barely speak. He swirled his tongue a few times, then coughed out, "I meant no harm. Lower your guns."

"Like hell," Clell said. "Back in the hills we'd kill a man for what you just did."

A new voice intruded, a voice with the ring of authority. "But you're not back in Tennessee, Mr.

Bowdrie. You're on my post, and what I say goes. So you will ease up on those hammers right this instant, or so help me God, not one of you will leave Fort Bowie alive. Not even your mongrel."

Col. Reynolds had rushed over with Capt. Forester, Sgt. McKinn, and half a dozen troopers in tow. He was taking no chances with men like the Bowdries. Six carbines and two pistols were trained on them. All he had to do was snap his fingers and they would be riddled where they stood.

Clem Bowdrie was no fool. His smooth features relaxed and he let the Sharps drop to his side. "Don't get your britches in an uproar, Colonel. All you have to do is hand over our money and we'll be out of your hair. And believe me, you'll never see us here again."

Reynolds glanced at the two brothers, who were much more reluctant to obey, but did. "I hope you will take this in the spirit in which it is meant," he said severely, "but nothing could please me more." He had seldom been more earnest. Reynolds couldn't wait for them to get off the post and out of his hair where they could do no more harm and cause him no more problems.

Or so the colonel thought.

Chapter Five

The roan went lame a day out from the Chiricahua Mountains. It surprised White Apache since he had not pushed the animal very hard. He reined up in a gully, checked its leg to verify it could not go on, and made the best of the situation by promptly slitting its throat.

Gathering dry wood did not take long. Soon White Apache had a fire crackling and a dripping slab of horse flesh on a makeshift spit over the leaping flames. He had not eaten a full meal in days and was going to indulge himself.

As an added treat, White Apache dug up small roots about the size of gooseberries and roasted them. Cuchillo Negro, a member of the renegade band, had taught him how to find the plant which produced the roots and many other tricks of surviving in the wild.

White Apache was careful to build his fire under

a cottonwood so that the little amount of smoke it gave off would be dispersed by the limbs. He felt perfectly safe. After all, he was in the middle of nowhere and had not seen another soul in days.

But unknown to him, a mile to the northwest a cavalry patrol led by Capt. Oliver Benteen was on its way back to Fort Bowie after making a wide sweep of the western approaches to the Chiricahuas.

Capt. Benteen had been on the frontier slightly over a year. Originally from a poor section of Philadelphia, he had entered the Army to get some schooling and see some of the country. He had no intention of making the military a career. In another two years his enlistment would be up and he planned to return to Pennsylvania and settle down.

Which explained why Benteen had a reputation for being overly cautious. Of all the officers under Col. Reynolds, he was the one least likely to engage renegades if he felt the enemy had the advantage. He claimed that he was only concerned for the welfare of the troopers under him, but his peers and his superior knew better. Capt. Oliver Benteen was concerned for his own hide above all else.

Col. Reynolds knew this. But he overlooked it. The colonel would much rather have an officer be too cautious than be too rash. The headstrong officers were the ones who got men needlessly killed.

And Benteen was highly competent. He discharged his duties better than any other officer at the post with the exception of Gerald Forester. To his further credit, he was also well liked by the Apache scouts since he was one of the few officers who treated them as equals. Whenever he had patrol duty, nearly every last one would volunteer to go along and he would have to pick the warrior he wanted.

On this particular patrol, the honor had fallen to a Jicarilla known as Antonio. In keeping with Apache custom, he never told the white-eyes his Jicarilla name, only the name by which the Mexicans called him. He was an older warrior, pushing fifty winters although he had the build and stamina of a man half his age.

Antonio had joined the Army as a scout for the same reason most Apaches did; reservation life had been unbearable. He had craved some measure of the adventure and excitement he had known before the coming of the whites. And the only way to do that, short of turning renegade, was to become a scout.

Now, as the patrol crested a knoll and rattled down the slope toward an arid plain, Antonio's eagle eyes were drawn to the southeast. He studied the sky a few moments, then slowed so the officer could catch up.

Capt. Benteen was riding beside his sergeant, a tough Irishman named Shawn O'Grady. They had been debating the merits of a certain schoolmarm in Tucson when Benteen saw his scout rise up and peer into the distance. From experience he knew what that meant and he immediately spurred his chestnut abreast of the Jicarilla.

"What is it, Antonio?"

"Little smoke," the warrior said in his heavily accented English. Pointing, he clarified its meaning in case the white-eye did not appreciate the difference, "Mean Indian fire."

Benteen nodded. It was common knowledge that white men were notorious for making their fires much too big, while Indians always made their fires small. "How far off is it?" he asked.

Antonio raised his hands and imitated shooting a bow. "Twenty flights of arrow. No more."

Capt. Benteen glanced back at the 28 troopers under his command. After two weeks of patrol they were all tired and dirty and keenly looking forward to getting back to Fort Bowie. But they had a job to do, and do it they would. Whipping his arm in an arc, he gave the order to advance at a trot. Sgt. O'Grady relayed it down the column and in moments the patrol was racing across the plain, Antonio in the lead.

Unaware of this development, White Apache hunkered over the roasting meat, savoring the aroma. There had been a time when his stomach would have churned at the notion of eating horse meat. To Apaches, though, it was a staple. A warrior never grew attached to a horse because he never knew when he might have to eat it. Since joining Delgadito's band, he had partaken many times.

White Apache's stomach growled. Impatient to eat, he drew his Bowie and carved off a fist-sized chunk. Hungrily he sank his teeth in deep and tore off a mouthful. Even half raw it tasted delicious. He wolfed the first bite and took another.

For over a minute White Apache chewed lustily. Flies were gathering around the dead roan and he could hear their buzzing clearly. He also heard a lizard slither through the brush to his left. Then, off in the distance, so faint that he almost missed it, a bird squawked.

White Apache paused in the act of tearing into the meat and glanced to the northwest. Once, he would have taken the sound for granted and figured a roving wildcat or some other animal had startled the bird. Not any more. An Apache never took anything for granted.

A red hawk soaring high over the mesquite to the west caught White Apache's eye. He watched it closely. He saw it bank to the northwest and make a series of loops as if examining something below. Moments later it veered off and climbed steeply, streaking due west.

White Apache rose, sheathed his knife, and wiped his greasy fingers on his legs. Picking up the Winchester, he dashed into the brush, turned to the north, and bounded like an antelope for over a hundred yards. On reaching a hillock which gave him a clear view of his camp, he flattened.

None too soon. Hooves thudded off through the chaparral. Tendrils of dust rose into the air. Soon riders materialized.

Antonio was still a few yards in the lead. Across his thighs rested his Henry. He spotted the dead horse and the fire at the same moment. Slowing to a walk, he elevated the rifle and scanned the vegetation beyond. He saw no one but he knew that he was being spied on.

Capt. Benteen raised his arm and the patrol likewise slowed. At a gesture, the column split in half and fanned out to the right and the left. Sgt. O'Grady rode at the head of the left line of troopers.

Benteen drew his Colt and made straight for the fire. The scent of roast horse meat hung ripe in the air. It made his stomach do flip-flops.

The Jicarilla halted beside the roan. Sliding down, he studied the hard earth carefully.

"How many?" Captain Benteen asked.

The scout did not answer. He was too intent on the tracks. There were few, mostly scuff marks and partial prints, but enough for a warrior of his ability to tell a great deal. And what he read in the dirt excited him beyond measure.

"How many, Antonio?" Benteen repeated.

"One," the Jicarilla disclosed. He came on a clear footprint and sank to one knee to better inspect it. His excitement mounted. "It be him."

Benteen nudged his horse closer. "Who?"

"The one they call White Apache."

The officer fairly flew off the chestnut and over beside the warrior. "Are you sure? We've had no reports of Taggart being in this area."

Antonio let the implied insult pass. Of course he was sure. He had learned to track when barely old enough to sit a saddle, and he was considered one of the best in his tribe. "See," he said, extending a finger and running it around the outline of the print. "Foot bend partway out."

"So?"

"So Indian foot bend in. White foot bend out. Man like White Apache, part white, part Indian, his foot bend partway out. Savvy?"

Benteen did, but he still had his doubts. It would be an incredible stroke of luck for him to have stumbled on Clay Taggart when the traitor was alone and on foot. Taggart's capture or elimination had been made the highest priority. Every officer in the Fifth Cavalry was under strict orders to be on the lookout for him, and to take whatever steps were necessary to bring the butcher's bloody reign of terror to an end. The officer glanced at the fire. "He can't have gone far."

Antonio looked up. "Him still here."

"What?"

"Him watch us. I feel it."

Capt. Benteen spun. "O'Grady! It's the White

Apache! Scour the brush! Check everywhere! He has to be nearby!"

The shout carried to Clay Taggart's ears and he promptly slid down the far side of the hillock, stood, and raced eastward. Threading through the prickly mesquite and dry weeds with a skill few white men could rival, he rapidly put as much ground behind him as he could.

Clay was not worried. Yet. It would take time for the scout to follow up his trail and determine which direction he had gone. By then he would change course. If he could elude them until nightfall, he'd be in the clear. Night, however, was hours off. He had his work cut out for him.

Pacing himself, White Apache ran at a tireless trot, just as the Chiricahuas had taught him. He grew thirsty but he shut his mind to the urge. Endurance, he had learned, was a state of mind. He had to close himself off to everything except the matter at hand. The simple act of moving his arms and legs and breathing in a regular rhythm took his full attention. That, and pricking his ears for sign of pursuit.

It came much sooner than White Apache had counted on. The crash of brush to the passage of horses and the jingle of cavalry accoutrements told him that the patrol had formed into a single long line and was pushing briskly eastward. They were no more than 500 feet away. Whoever was in charge knew all the tricks.

Capt. Benteen liked to think that he did. He rode at the center of the line with the Jicarilla on his right and the sergeant on his left. His intent was to flush the traitor and surround him. If Taggart resisted, the man would be shot to pieces. If not, then Benteen stood to become the envy of every officer in the Southwest. The man who brought in the White Apache would become famous. It would be written up in all the newspapers. A promotion would be in the offing, and Benteen liked the idea of being a major. If he played his cards right, he could be a full colonel in five years. The possibility was sufficient to give him second thoughts about civilian life.

Antonio had his head bent to the ground. Every now and then he would see a smudge or some other trace of their quarry. They were very close behind. He curled his thumb around the hammer of his Henry, certain the white-eye would put up a fight.

Nor was he alone in thinking that. Sgt. O'Grady had been involved in several Indian campaigns. He had fought the Sioux on the high plains. He had tangled with the Comanches in Texas. Apaches, in his opinion, were little different, only tougher and meaner. Through all his campaigns, he had stayed alive because he always stayed alert and he was wise enough to anticipate what the enemy would do before the enemy would do it.

In this instance, O'Grady was certain the traitor would open fire if they got too close. He probed the undergrowth ahead, his carbine held loosely in his brawny hands. His marksmanship was superb, the talk of the post. As the troopers liked to say, "If O'Grady can see it, he can hit it." All Clay Taggart had to do was show himself and he was a dead man.

But Clay had no such intention. The onrushing soldiers were 300 feet to the west when he came to a dry wash. Bearing to the right for 40 feet, he hopped down off the shallow bank, set his rifle to one side, and clawed at the loose earth as if he were an oversized prairie dog trying to dig a burrow. Which, in effect, he was.

Trackers

Clay had learned from masters how to use terrain to his advantage. He was adept at blending into the background, at bending his body into the shape of boulders and bushes, at disguising himself with branches and grass and dirt.

The earth gave way quickly. He scooped out a hole just large enough for him to squeeze into, and did so. The Winchester went across his body. By then the patrol was so close that the ground rumbled. He pulled the loose dirt back in after him, covering himself but leaving a small hole to see through. As he finished, thunder peeled above him. Fine particles of dust rained onto his face and neck. He had to stifle an impulse to sneeze.

A shadow swooped across the wash, preceding a soldier who vaulted his horse off the bank and galloped to the other side. Clay saw several of them, including the scout and the officer, off to the left. They rode on up the opposite bank without looking back. The second that the line of blue coats disappeared, he pushed the dirt off him, squeezed out, sprang to the top of the bank, and sped off in the direction he had come.

It would not fool the scout for long, Clay knew. He had to think of something else. But what?

Outwitting an Apache took some doing. Erasing his tracks with a tree limb would do no good since the marks made by the leaves would be a dead giveaway. Nor would it help if he tried to walk backward in his own footsteps for a while. Any tracker worthy of the name knew that when a man did that the steps were shorter and the heel marks were deeper than they should be.

One ruse would buy him a little extra time, and that was to travel through the thickest of the mesquite. It would slow the cavalrymen down since they would not risk harming their mounts.

After a few minutes White Apache turned to the south. In the distance reared a bluff. From its crown he would be able to see the patrol. He went faster, wondering if the troopers were wise to his ruse yet.

They were. Antonio realized that he had lost the scent after traveling 60 yards past the wash. He told Benteen, who ordered the troop to swing around and search for sign. The Jicarilla tried to put himself in the moccasins of the white-eye renegade, to think what he would do if he were the one being chased. When he saw the wash, he understood, and he smiled at White Apache's cleverness.

The freshly dug hole was obvious to everyone. Antonio showed where the man had plunged back into the chaparral. Once again the troopers spread out in a long line and advanced at the double. Every man sensed that they were closing in. Their carbines were at the ready.

Capt. Benteen was growing worried that the traitor would elude them. The man had the wiles of a fox. And he was certainly no coward. It had taken great courage to lie in that small hole, unable to even bring a gun to bear to defend himself, while the patrol galloped on past above him. If just one trooper had spotted it, Taggart would have been trapped with no way out. Benteen knew himself well enough to admit that he would never have been able to do the same thing.

Sgt. O'Grady was making it a point to stay close to the officer. He recollected hearing that in several prior clashes with the cavalry, the White Apache had picked off those in charge at the outset. The man was no fool. Taggart knew that dropping the officers and noncoms would throw the privates into confusion and give him time to make his escape. Well, O'Grady was not about to let that happen this time.

Suddenly the brush to the northwest crackled. A nervous soldier opened fire, banging off four shots before he saw that it was a deer, not Clay Taggart. The buck was struck twice high in the chest and died on its feet.

White Apache heard the shots and paused. They helped him pinpoint the patrol, and he was disturbed to discover that the cavalrymen had caught on to his trick and were hot on his heels again. Or, rather, their scout had. He resumed his course toward the bluff at twice the speed.

It dawned on Clay that perhaps this time his luck had run out. Perhaps he had met his match in this scout. He might never reach Sweet Grass, the Chiricahua sanctuary high in the rugged mountain range of the same name. He might never get to take his full revenge on Miles Gillett and Lilly.

That last notion, more than any other, fired him with new resolve. Clay was not going to let the soldiers take him without a fight they would long remember. He skirted a small cactus and had a clear path to the base of the bluff, which reared over 50 feet above the sea of mesquite.

Antonio, meanwhile, had lost the trail again. He bore wide in both directions seeking more tracks but could find none. Capt. Benteen gazed at him expectantly, and Antonio could tell that the officer was upset. But what else could he do? he asked himself. The mesquite rose as high as his shoulder in places.

Inspiration struck when the warrior saw a sparrow perched on a limb. Reining up, he patted the neck of his pinto a few times to steady the animal, then he coiled his legs to his chest, placed his feet flat on the saddle, and unlimbered to his full height of five feet, seven inches, balancing on the balls of his feet. It pleased him that the officer and the nearest troopers gawked. They would tell of his deed back at the fort and his worth would rise in the eyes of the other white-eyes.

Suddenly Antonio glimpsed a figure in a breechcloth flitting through the brush to the south. It had to be the White Apache, and he was almost to a high bluff. "I see him," Antonio declared, sinking back down. "He is not far."

Unaware that he had been seen, Clay Taggart started up the gradual barren slope. Gullies and crevices laced the face of the bluff, offering ample places to hide. He passed several ideal spots on his climb to the top. Halfway up, as Clay rose onto a narrow bench, he glanced over a shoulder and felt his gut tighten into a knot as hard as the quartz which veined the bluff.

The patrol was converging on him.

Clay glanced down, his mind racing. In the time it took him to climb back to the bottom, the troopers would reach the base and cut him off. His best bet lay in getting up and over the other side before they pinned him down. To that end he scrambled higher. He had less than ten feet to go to gain the summit.

Then Clay reached up, wedged his right hand into a crack, and went to pull himself higher still. Without warning the earth around the crack crumbled and gave way, throwing him backward. He tried to dig in his heels. He tried to snatch hold of a rocky spine. Gravity conspired against him and he tumbled, raising a cloud of dust and bloodthirsty cheers from the charging troopers who believed that his blunder put him at their mercy.

And maybe they were right.

White Apache landed with a jarring impact on the bench. As he rose to his knees shots rang out. Lead thudded into the bluff on both sides of him. Some of the soldiers had broken from cover and were firing on the fly. Snapping the Winchester to his shoulder, he fixed a bead on the foremost trooper and shot the man right out of the saddle. Shifting, he worked the lever, feeding a new cartridge into the chamber. His second shot caught a burly cavalryman in the forehead and catapulted the man over the rump of his mount as if he had been fired from a slingshot.

Capt. Benteen was beside himself. He had been yelling for his men to take cover but a half-dozen or so ignored him in their excitement and eagerness to kill the scourge of the Territory. In an effort to get their attention, he raked his horse with his spurs and began to pull ahead of them, shouting all the while, "Cease firing! Take cover!"

Sgt. O'Grady had fallen a dozen feet behind his superior. On seeing the officer race madly into the open, fear coursed through him. He called out, "Sir! Stop! Get under cover yourself!" But his yell went unheard in the general din. Glancing toward the bluff, he saw the White Apache in the act of taking aim. Instantly O'Grady fired three times as fast as he could.

The shots came closer than any so far to nailing Clay Taggart. Two whizzed past his cheek. The third smacked into the dirt inches above his head. Clay paid them no heed. He had spotted the officer in charge of the patrol. Hastily aligning his sights, he held his breath a moment, then stroked the trigger.

To Capt. Benteen, it felt as if a red-hot poker had seared his ribs. He knew he had been hit and placed a hand on his side. When he drew the hand away it was covered with blood. Dizziness assailed him.

Suddenly Sgt. Shawn O'Grady was there. Looping a well-muscled arm around the officer, he guided Benteen's horse into the mesquite to the east. The rest of the patrol followed their cue.

Up on the bluff, Clay Taggart ran out of targets. He spied a wide cleft nearby and threw himself into it as a ragged volley peppered the bench. When the volley faded, he peeked above the rim. The troopers were swiftly ringing the bluff. In another minute they would have it surrounded.

He was trapped.

Chapter Six

His name was Santiago Pasqual. In his opinion the greatest affliction in his life was to have been born of a Mexican mother and a Cibeque father. This made him a halfbreed. And breeds, sad to say, were held in little regard by both whites and their full-blooded Indian brethren.

Santiago hated being looked down on as some sort of two-legged cur. He despised Americanos and full-bloods alike, no matter which tribe they belonged to. Apaches, Pimas, Maricopas, it made no difference. Secretly he loathed them all.

Secretly, because it would not do for word to get out. Apaches were notoriously touchy about such things. He might wake up in the middle of the night some time with his throat slit from ear to ear. Or he might lose all his customers, which would put him out of business. And he did love his work.

Santiago owned a run-down saloon which in

most other parts of the United States would have been condemned as a hovel. It sat just over the boundary line of the Chiricahua Reservation, not all that far from Fort Bowie.

Most of those who came daily to drown their sorrows in red-eye were Apaches. Even though it was against the law, the Chiricahuas didn't care. Many were addicted to the firewater of the white-eyes. They could no more get through a day without a drink or three than they could without breathing.

Many Mexicans also made Santiago's their favorite watering hole, since it was one of the few places they could go to drink where they did not have to put up with arrogant gringos. Not usually, at any rate, for there were times when Americanos did stop by.

This day was one of them. Santiago stood at the bar, idly polishing a dirty glass with a grimy rag. Only seven customers were present, scattered about the dingy room. In the back, Santiago's woman toiled over a hot stove, making burritos and enchiladas and other tasty dishes for those who were hungry. He could hear her hum as she worked, and he smiled, thinking of her ample posterior.

Then there rose an odd scraping noise at the front door. Santiago looked up, and his breath caught in his throat. For a moment he thought that he must be seeing things.

Framed in the doorway was a creature that appeared to be something out of Santiago's worst nightmare. It was half the size of a bear but had the head of a wolf and a coat as shaggy as a buffalo's. Piercing eyes raked the saloon as if seeking its next meal. Santiago set down the glass and started to reach under the counter for the scatter-gun he kept handy to deal with rowdy drunks. He froze, though, when a buckskin-clad form appeared beside the strange beast.

Santiago recognized that form, and the other two who filed in behind him and over to a corner table. Their mongrel monster stayed at their side even though there was a sign out front, in both English and Spanish, warning that no dogs were permitted inside. Santiago had written the sign himself.

Inwardly cursing all whites for thinking they had the God-given right to do as they damn well pleased, Pasqual plastered a smile on his swarthy face and walked over. He pretended not to notice when the shaggy creature fixed a baleful glare on him and growled.

"That's enough out of you, Razor," Clem Bowdrie said. "You be civil, you hear?"

Tick Bowdrie snickered. "Aw, let the dog have some fun. He ain't gnawed on anyone in days."

Santiago recalled hearing somewhere that animals could smell when a man was afraid. In that case, the monster squatting by the table had to know that he was terrified to the bone. But he did not let on. For the benefit of his regular customers, he put on a brave front and said, "*Hola*, senors. It has been a long time since last you graced my humble establishment."

Clell Bowdrie thumped his Winchester down on the table top. "Lordy, Pasqual. You're still as full of it as you ever were. Don't you ever get tired of pickin' all that brown stuff out of your ears?"

Acting as if he did not know what the gringo meant, Santiago asked, "What will it be today, my friends?"

"We ain't your friends, you greasy breed," Tick declared. "Just bring us three bottles of coffin varnish. And none of that watered down stuff you sell the Injuns, neither. Not if you want to stay healthy."

Santiago's resentment knew no bounds. But he was not about to court death by giving the Americanos a piece of his mind. "Whiskey it is," he said pleasantly. "I will be right back."

The Bowdries sullenly watched the proprietor hurry off, and Tick Bowdrie snorted. "I can't stand a man who grovels. One of these days I might just put him out of his misery and blow out his brains."

"It'd be a waste of good lead," Clell commented. Leaning back and staring at the other customers with blatant contempt. "What the hell did we come here for, anyhow? I hate drinkin' with Injuns and breeds."

"It was handy," Clem said, "and I had me a powerful hankerin'. After the way those Army sons of bitches treated us, I'm burnin' up inside."

Tick leaned his Spencer against the adobe wall. "Uppity bastards. Actin' as if they're better than everyone else. And after we went and brought back them deserters just like they wanted." He shook his head. "Some folks have no gratitude, you know that?"

Over behind the bar, Santiago Pasqual took three bottles of his best stock and placed them on a tray. He was tempted to water them down just a little out of sheer spite, but he dared not take the risk. The Bowdries were not men to trifle with. Them with their smelly clothes and dirty faces.

As Santiago came around the end of the bar, he noticed something strange, something he had never noticed before. It surprised him so much that he broke stride.

Only two of the three Bowdries were greasy and dirty. Clell and Tick looked as if they had just crawled out of a pigpen after wrestling a boar. But the third one, Clem, the one with that peculiar hat, was smooth-shaven and clean, as were his baggy buckskins. The contrast was so striking that Santiago was amazed he had never spotted it before. Normally he was quite observant.

"Here you go, senors," Pasqual said as he lowered the tray. "Is there anything else I can get you? Food, perhaps? My Teresina can make tacos like you have never tasted before."

"We don't want no greaser food," Tick replied gruffly. "Just keep the tarantula juice comin' and we'll be right happy."

"As you wish," Santiago said, wishing he could stick the muzzle of his scattergun into the swine of a gringo's mouth and pull the trigger. He smiled at Clell and Clem and went to turn when his gaze happened to drift to the level of the table top. He blinked in astonishment, then quickly hastened away before they saw, thinking that it couldn't be, that he must be mistaken.

Once safely behind the bar, Santiago made it a point not to pay any attention to them. They drank and muttered among themselves while their creature dozed.

Perhaps an hour had gone by. Perhaps two. Santiago was not one for keeping track of time. He was about to partake of a bowl of beans when the drum of many hooves outside let him know he was about to have more customers. Whoever they were, they were in a hurry. He guessed there must be five or six of them, and he wondered what could be so important that they would push their horses so hard during the hottest part of the day.

Boots stomped toward the door. Spurs jangled loudly. Santiago faced around to welcome the new-

79

comers but shock turned his tongue to stone. He thought for certain that he had somehow offended his Maker and was being punished for his transgression. For as if it were not bad enough that the vile Bowdries had seen fit to pay his humble saloon a visit, now into his establishment came men every bit as dangerous.

First to enter was a young man whose smooth, babylike features belied his deadly nature. Billy Santee wore a wide-brimmed black hat and twin gunbelts crossed over his slim hips. He was the single most infamous gunman in the Territory and proud of it.

Next came a man whose reputation was almost the equal of Santee's own. Surgio Vasquez had on a high-crowned sombrero and fancy Mexican garb. His oversized rowels jingled as he stepped to one side to survey the room.

More gunmen entered. Four, all told. Three of them Santiago had seen before but he did not know their names. The fourth was a lean stranger with the features of a hawk and an expensive pearl-handled Colt worn butt forward on his left side.

Then the entrance was filled from lintel to doorstep by an enormous man as wide as he was tall. He wore a brown suit and pressed white shirt and a hat which had cost as much as Santiago made in a month. Unlike the others, he did not wear a gun. He did not need to. The man himself radiated raw power and menace, much as might a giant grizzly.

Santiago Pasqual was flabbergasted. He knew this man. Not to talk to, but by the many stories told about him. Straightening, he forced his mouth to move, saying, "Senor Gillett! This is a surprise! How may I be of service?"

Miles Gillett was not one to waste words or time.

"You can't," he said curtly, and stalked over to the table where the Bowdrie brothers sat.

The Tennesseans were as taken aback by the arrival of the wealthy rancher as everyone else, but they did not let on. Clem studied the gunmen and seemed to find the hawk-faced man interesting.

"We need to talk," Gillett announced. Taking a chair from another table and twirling it, he eased down, resting his powerful forearms on the top brace. The gunmen fanned out to surround their employer. "You know who I am and I know who you are, so we can cut to the reason I'm here."

Tick Bowdre shifted. He did not like being hemmed in by so many gun sharks and had half a mind to tell them to back off. But, as always, he would follow Clem's lead, and Clem just sat there smiling. "Yep, I reckon we do know you, mister," he answered. "Everyone in Arizona does."

"I've been looking all over for the three of you," Gillett revealed. He removed his hat as he spoke and took a clean handkerchief from his jacket pocket to wipe his sweaty brow. "We just missed running into you at Fort Bowie. Col. Reynolds pointed us in the right direction."

"Damn decent of the blue-belly, seein' as how he hates our guts," Clell mentioned. "But why would a big, important man like you need to see poor white trash like us so badly?" He nodded at Razor. "Are you in the market for one of them there pedigree dogs?"

Miles Gillett did not laugh. "Listen to me, you peckerwood. I didn't damn near ride one of my best horses into the ground just to listen to you flap your gums." He focused on Clem. "I hear that you're the brains of the family."

The blond found that highly amusing. "Ain't it the

81

truth. The brains and the looks. But don't slight Tick and Clell none. What they don't have between the ears they more than make up for in pure grit."

Gillett nodded. "The three of you are supposed to be the best at what you do. Which is why I'm willing to pay ten-thousand dollars for the job I want done. Half now, half when it's over with."

Clem's mouth dropped, and the others were just as flustered. "Ten thousand? Lord Almighty, we ain't never seen that much money in all our born days." Those wary blue eyes narrowed. "You must want us to go after someone awful special if you're willin' to fork over a king's ransom. Who the hell is it? The President of these here United States?"

A grin touched the huge man's lips. "Killing the President would be easier than the job I have for you." He paused. "I want you to bring me the head of Clay Taggart, and I don't care how you get it."

"Taggart?" Clem repeated. "Ain't he that White Apache feller? The one the whole blamed cavalry can't catch?"

Clell whistled. "You're askin' a lot, mister. Taggart rides with Delgadito's bunch. Those red devils are pure terrors. If we go after him, we might have to go up against the whole band of renegades."

"Don't tell me that you're scared of a few measly Apaches?" Gillett baited him. "And here everyone claims that the Bowdrie boys aren't afraid of anyone or anything."

The taunt riled Clell, who leaned forward and made as if to slap the rancher. Lightning quick, Clem grabbed the other Bowdrie's wrist, then shoved his arm flat, saying with a meaningful nod at the gunmen, "Don't be stupid."

Billy Santee, Surgio Vasquez and all the other gunnies had tensed, except for the man with the hawkish countenance. He alone lounged against a wall, giving the impression he didn't have a care in the world.

Clem looked Gillett in the eyes. "You won't get nowhere insultin' us, mister. It's true that we're not afeared of any man alive. But we're not dumb, neither. Anyone would think twice about settin' his sights on Taggart and those renegades."

"Which is why I'm offering so much to have him taken care of," Gillett said. "He's been a thorn in my side long enough. After the other night—" He caught himself and let the words trail off.

"Taggart raid your place, did he?" Clem asked.

The rancher nodded curtly. "He killed my prize bull," was all he had to say on the subject. But one of his own men had more.

Billy Santee tittered like a boy of ten. "That's not all the varmint did. He cut the head clean off and then lugged it into the boss's house. Right into the bedroom!" The young gunman slapped his thigh in merriment. "Can you imagine the sheer gall! What would make a man think to do such a thing?"

Clem's brow knit. "It does give a body cause to wonder, don't it?"

"Wonder all you want to," Gillett said harshly. "But I need to know now if you'll take the job or not. If you won't, I'll go find someone who will. One way or the other Clay Taggart is a dead man. I promised my wife that he'll be dead before the first frost and I mean to keep my word."

"A man should always stick by his promises to a lady," Clem said with an impish smirk. "I know I would."

Gillett did not take kindly to the remark and it showed. "Be real careful, mister. No one pokes fun at my wife, ever. The last hombre who did had to go out later and buy himself a set of false teeth."

"I meant no disrespect," Clem said, unbowed. "Believe you me, no one thinks more highly of womenfolk than I do." The statement rang sincere, but it didn't help matters any that Clell and Tick both chuckled to themselves and made of a show of finding the ceiling interesting.

The rancher made a sharp gesture. "Enough. What's your decision? Will you take the job or not?" His hand slipped under his jacket and came out holding a wad of bills as thick as his wrist. "I have five-thousand right here. The rest is yours when you hand over Taggart's head."

Tick and Clell sobered and stared at the money as starving men might at a turkey dinner with all the trimmings. "I declare," the former said. "Look at all that!"

"But it ain't coin money," Clell noted.

"I reckon we can make an exception this time around," Clem remarked, and extended a palm. "All right, Mr. Gillett. You have yourself a deal. The Bowdries will fetch this White Apache. Once we've taken up his scent, he's as good as done for."

Miles Gillett tossed the wad into the air and caught it. "Before I hand this over, there is one condition I must insist on, given the circumstances."

"Uh-oh," Tick said. "Why is it the ones with lots of money always get so darned fussy about how we do our work? Seems to me a body ought to have a little faith."

"With this much of my money at stake, I think I have a perfect right to impose on your good will," Gillett said suavely. "Besides, the condition is a simple one. All you have to do is take one of my men along with you."

The Bowdries glanced at one another, displeased.

Clem voiced the thought they all shared. "We work by ourselves. Always have. Always will."

"Not this time. Not if you want the ten grand. I want someone along to sort of keep an eye on my investment. If it's too much of an imposition, just say so."

"It is," Clell said flatly.

"Damned tootin'," Tick agreed. "We don't need no nursemaid along. If you don't trust us, you should never have looked us up in the first place."

Gillett ignored them. He concentrated on Clem, stressing, "It's just one man. What harm can that do? And to make the pill easier to swallow, I'll send another Southerner." Twisting, he jabbed a thick thumb at the man with the pearl-handled Colt. "His name is Vasco."

The lean gunman lost his casual air. Standing straight, he drawled, "The hell you say, seh. This wasn't part of our arrangement. I hired on to throw lead for you, not be no nursemaid. Get yourself another gent."

"You hired on to do as I say," Miles Gillett countered. "Any man who takes my money and won't do as I want can collect his pay and light a shuck for all I care. The choice is yours. But I figured you to have enough sand to handle anything I throw your way."

A critical moment had arrived. Clell and Tick sneered at the gunman as if daring him to accept, while Vasco opened his mouth apparently to refuse. Just then, Clem Bowdrie surprised everyone by piping up with, "Very well, mister. We Bowdries agree to your terms. Any jasper who fancies such a shiny Colt must be mighty fast on the draw. He's bound to come in handy."

Tick Bowdrie was stupefied. "He is? Since when?

What the blazes has gotten into you, Clem? I'm sorry, but I'm buckin' you on this one. We don't need no outsider ridin' with us."

Clell Bowdrie had glanced closely at Clem, then at Vasco. A thoughtful expression came over him. "Well now," he said quietly, "ordinarily I'd agree with brother Tick, but seein' as how you want it so much, Clem, I reckon I'll go along with you. This feller can tag along. But heed me. He'd best not get in our way."

"It's settled then," Miles Gillett said, and gave the five thousand to Clem.

Santiago Pasqual had been a fascinated eavesdropper to the whole conversation. In his line of work information was sometimes more valuable than the finest whiskey he sold, so he had learned to keep his eyes and ears open at all times. He did not see how he could make much money off this newest development, but there was no doubt that it would be the talk of the Territory for the next few weeks.

Miles Gillett stood. "When it's over, bring the head to my ranch. Vasco will guide you there." He turned to go, then drew up short. "Oh. One more thing. You might like to know that when Taggart left my spread the other night, he headed due east. And he was alone. My guess is that he was making for the Chiricahuas. Rumor has it that's where the renegades hole up. If you hurry, you might be able to pick up his trail while it's fresh." Pivoting, the big man hustled on out and his men filed along behind him.

Billy Santee looked as if he were about to make a sarcastic comment, but something in Vasco's eyes changed his mind and he sauntered off with only a wink and a grin.

In the silence which ensued, anyone could have heard a pin drop.

Vasco walked over to the table and stood staring down at Clem Bowdrie. "Why?" he asked at length. "What made you change your mind?"

"I thought I made it plain. We're goin' up against redskins, ain't we? We can always use another gun." Clem stood, hefted the Sharps, and brushed past the gunman. "Tick, you pay what we owe for our drinks, you hear?"

Clell and a mystified Vasco trailed him outdoors.

Scratching his head in confusion, Tick Bowdrie came over to the bar and plucked a handful of coins from a pocket. "If I live to be a hundred, I will never understand Clem," he muttered.

"I feel the same way about my Teresina," Santiago said. "But that is life, *si*? There are some things it is given a man to comprehend and there are some things which are not."

"I don't recollect askin' you," Tick said. He was in a foul mood, and with good cause. Between the blue-bellies giving them a hard time about the deserters and now the high and mighty Miles Gillett all but forcing a new job down their throats, he was fit to be tied. Nothing that day had gone as it should.

As was often the case when he became irritated, Tick felt an urge to pound on something. Or someone. He half hoped the barkeep would give him an excuse to resort to his fists, but he should have known better. Pasqual was as slick as axle grease.

"How right you are, senor. Please forgive me for speaking when I should not have. I trust you will not hold it against me."

Tick had a hunch he was being played for a fool

but he could not say exactly how. "You're forgiven, breed," he snapped, and paid for the whiskey. "If we don't set eyes on you for a year or so, it'll be too soon to suit me." Satisfied in his parting shot, he went out the door in a rush. The others, including Vasco, were mounted.

"Let's go," Clem said. "Daylight is wastin' away. We can cover a lot of ground before dark comes."

Swinging onto his mule without saying a word, Tick saw the older Bowdrie give Vasco a broad smile. Clell, meanwhile, was grinning at a private joke. None of it made any sense to Tick. He would be as happy as a lark when the whole affair was over with and they could go on about their lives as they had before that miserable day began.

Except for being ten-thousand dollars richer.

Chapter Seven

A whole day had gone by.

Capt. Oliver Benteen propped himself on an elbow to peer over the mound of earth which screened him from the bluff. The exertion lanced his side with pain. Grunting, he automatically pressed a hand to the makeshift bandage which covered the deep furrow across his ribs.

"Better take it easy, sir," Sgt. Shawn O'Grady cautioned. "You don't want to open that wound again."

The officer glanced at the big Irishman. "All you need to do is sprout feathers and a beak and you would make a fine mother hen, Sergeant."

O'Grady grinned. He would be the first to admit that he had been hovering over Benteen like a hawk. But that was what he got paid for. The welfare of every member of the patrol was his foremost priority. Nodding at the bluff, he asked, "Do you reckon the bastard is still up there, sir?"

"I don't see how he could have slipped away without us noticing," Benteen replied. It had been close to six hours since the White Apache had last made his presence known. A private named Wilcox had made the mistake of exposing a leg and Taggart had put a slug into the young man's ankle. Wilcox would live but he might be crippled for life.

Benteen shifted to somberly stare at the blanket covered bodies lying 40 feet away, near the horses. Two troopers had been killed so far and three wounded, counting himself. But he was not about to give up. Not when he still had twenty-five able-bodied men still at his disposal and they had the terror of the Southwest completely hemmed in.

Time was on Benteen's side. The White Apache had no food up there, no water. Soon the renegade would begin to feel the effects of the blistering heat. All Benteen had to do was sit tight and be ready when Clay Taggart made a break for it.

There was a whisper of movement and suddenly Antonio was next to them, materializing out of the mesquite as if out of thin air. He squatted, his Henry across his legs, as impassive as a statue.

"Any luck?" Benteen asked. Half an hour ago he had sent the Apache to scour the bluff from top to bottom in the hope that the scout would spot Taggart.

"No," Antonio regretted having to report. He had always prided himself on his exceptionally keen eyesight, but it had failed him this time. He had looked and looked and not seen any trace of their quarry. The White Apache, he reflected, was a credit to his name.

"So what do we do, sir?" Sgt. O'Grady asked. "Wait him out?"

"Exactly," Benteen confirmed. Twisting, he

probed the chaparral and spotted several members of the patrol. They were strung out at regular intervals, completely circling the bluff. It would be impossible for so much as a jackrabbit to get past them without being spotted.

Scattered here and there were the charred remains of the huge brush fires Benteen had ordered made the evening before. All night long the troopers had kept the fires going, lighting up the base of the bluff as brightly as day. Benteen had been sure that Taggart would try to slip away but the night had passed quietly. Too quietly. He had begun to worry that perhaps Taggart had already given them the slip. Then Pvt. Wilcox had been shot.

Now, staring up at the seamed slope, Benteen wondered what was going through the mind of the White Apache. It was rumored that Taggart had pledged never to be taken alive. Would the man carry out his vow? Would Taggart go out in a blaze of gunfire, or would he weaken and give up?

One thing was for sure. Benteen was glad that he wasn't in Clay Taggart's boots. No matter what the man did, he was as good as dead. If Taggart surrendered, he would be taken back for trial. Public sentiment being what it was, they would hold a public hanging and folks would come from hundreds of miles around to witness the end of the man who had terrorized them for so long. It would be like that time in Colorado Territory when thousands showed up for a hanging and turned the ghastly event into a virtual holiday.

A hand touched Benteen's arm. Antonio pointed to the west and said, "Trouble come."

The officer looked. All he saw was a solitary cloud low on the horizon. "What kind of trouble?" he inquired.

"Much rain."

Benteen scanned the sky from north to south. "You must be mistaken," he said, and regretted it when the Jicarilla frowned. "I don't mean to doubt you, Antonio. But how do you know? What do you see that I don't?"

The warrior tapped the tip of his nose with a bronzed finger. "Not see. Smell. Heavy rain come before sun set. Thunder. Lightning." Antonio bobbed his chin toward the bluff. "Him know, I bet. Him be glad to see rain come."

The aged scout was right. White Apache had caught the faint but dank scent of the oncoming storm system sometime ago. He had sat up and peered westward, trying to gauge how long it would be before the downpour hit. But he could not tell.

A true Chiricahua would know. A full-blooded warrior learned to read the moods of Nature as white men read the printed pages of books. Early on in life a warrior was taught by his elders how to tell the different types of clouds and what each type meant. He was taught to use his nose to a degree white men rarely did. He learned, in effect, to attune his senses to the rhythms of the wild.

Clay Taggart could do the same, although not nearly as well. To other white men his abilities might seem uncanny. To the Chiricahuas, however, he was somewhat backward, a grown man who handled himself about as well as a fourteen or fifteen-year old Apache might.

Clay knew his limits and he did not try to exceed them. He did constantly work at improving himself, at becoming better at the many skills at which the Chiricahuas excelled. One day he would be their equal, or as close to being one as any white man had ever been or ever would be.

Settling back, Clay surveyed the mesquite below. The troopers were well hidden. Not so their horses. Northeast of the bluff several were partly visible, and he made a mental note of the spot for later on.

To while away the time, Clay checked his .44-40 Winchester to verify he had a full fifteen rounds in the magazine. He also checked his .45-caliber single-action Colt. Both guns took the new metallic center-fire cartridges which were a distinct improvement over the older linen and paper cartridges and the flimsy rim-fires.

A while back there had been talk in Tucson that at some point down the road the Colt company planned to put out a pistol which could take the same cartridge as the Winchester rifle. Most frontiersmen could hardly wait. It would mean a great savings in weight and money to be able to use the same ammunition in both. Instead of having to tote two cartridge belts, a man would only need one.

Clay also took out his Bowie and wiped the blade clean of dust on his breechcloth. Next he hiked his moccasins to his knees and looped strands of rawhide around the tops to hold them in place. He was now as ready as he would ever be.

A loud rumble came from Clay's stomach. He ignored it, even though he was hungry enough to eat horse meat raw. He also ignored his parched throat. Taking a pebble off the ground, he stuck it under his tongue. The pebble would make his mouth water and keep it moist, yet another trick he had learned from the Chiricahuas. It would have to suffice until he found some water.

The day dragged on. More and more clouds appeared. The scent of rain grew steadily stronger. Clay wondered if the cavalrymen knew they were in for a gully-washer, and if they would take steps to keep him from slipping off when the thunderstorm hit. He saw no evidence of movement and figured they had no idea.

But he was wrong. Capt. Benteen no longer had any doubts about Antonio's prediction. Motioning for O'Grady to come closer, he gave new orders.

"Make the rounds of the men. Tell them to expect Taggart to try to escape during the height of the storm. Advise them to be ready to move out at my signal."

"Sir?"

"The rain will work in our favor as well as his. He won't be able to pick us off if he can't see us. Once the rain is heavy enough, we can work our way right up to the bottom of the bluff without him being any the wiser." Benteen patted his pistol. "I'll fire a shot into the air. That will be the signal for the men to advance and surround the bluff at close range. If we're practically rubbing elbows, there's no way in hell Taggart will be able to sneak past us."

The sergeant grinned. "An excellent plan, sir, if I do say so myself." Staying bent at the waist, he hastened off to do as he had been told.

Again a hand brushed the officer's wrist.

"Where you want me?" Antonio asked.

"You're free to do as you want," Benteen said. According to regulations, a scout was sent with every patrol to do just that. When it came to actual fighting, the Army preferred for regular troops to engage the enemy. Many officers would have it no other way. While they trusted the scouts to hunt the rogues down, most officers secretly harbored grave doubts that the scouts would wholeheartedly take to slaying fellow Apaches.

The Jicarilla nodded, then melted into the underbrush. He knew where he could do them the most good. The captain had not thought of everything.

Up on the bluff, Clay Taggart spied movement and brought the Winchester to bear. No sooner had he fixed a bead on a shadowy figure in blue than the figure blended into the chaparral. He kept the rifle pressed to his shoulder, thinking that the trooper might soon reappear. But minutes went by and no one showed.

Meanwhile, clouds continued to gather to the west. Within the hour a dark bank of them roiled over a full third of the sky. It would not be long before they swooped down over the bluff.

White Apache inched to the lip of the cleft to study the slope below. Once the downpour began, he would not be able to see more than a few feet in front of him. He needed to memorize the location of any and all obstacles he would encounter on the way down so he could avoid them.

There was a crevice ten feet lower. Below that, boulders littered a wide area. Further down, cracks and ruts and a tangle of weeds would slow him down.

The wind grew steadily stronger. Soon it whipped off the slope in mighty gusts, whirling tendrils of dust into the air and bending the weeds as if they were so much straw. The mesquite shook to the blasts of chill air, rustling noisily.

More and more dark clouds flashed eastward. Far to the west thunder rumbled. Occasionally; Clay glimpsed ragged bolts of lightning in the distance. The scent of rain was now so strong that it made his craving for water twice as intense as before. He smacked his dry lips, eager for the first drops to fall.

Another half an hour went by. Finally it happened. Clay heard a soft plop to his left, another to his right. Something moist and cold struck him on the right shoulder. He turned his head. A tiny drop rested on his skin. Touching the tip of a finger to it, he licked the water off, then smiled.

Drops fell with greater frequency. Mixed with them were small hailstones which pummeled the mesquite like buckshot. The rattle of the stones was like the grating of gravel on tin.

Shrieking like a banshee, the wind grew even worse. Clay's body broke out in goosebumps. He shivered. Moving to the right, he pressed close to a break in the cleft just wide enough for him to slip through. It would not be long now, he told himself. Nature was coming to his rescue.

Thunder rumbled ever louder. Increasing numbers of vivid bolts ruptured the sky. One struck less than a quarter-of-a-mile off with a bright flash and a crackle that pricked the short hairs at the nape of Clay's neck. He tilted his head back and opened his mouth wide as the rain commenced coming down in earnest.

Seldom had any water tasted so delicious as that which Clay gulped down. It was just enough to quench his thirst but not enough to satisfy his craving. Soon the rain fell in sheets. He was soaked from head to toe, but he hardly cared.

Clay peeked around the break. The base of the bluff was completely shrouded by the deluge. He could descend with impunity. Slipping onto the slope, he carefully worked his way downward. So heavy was the downpour that already the slope had become like glass. One misstep and he would pay the consequences.

When Clay suspected that he was close to the

crevice, he sank onto his hands and knees and crawled forward. His left hand poked into thin air. Drawing back, he roved his finger along the edge, getting his bearings. As he recollected, the crevice was about four-feet wide. Under normal conditions he could leap it with ease.

Kneeling at the rim, Clay slowly rose. The rain had become a liquid wall. He could barely see his hand when he held it six-inches from his face. And the other side of the crevice was a blur. Girding himself, he coiled his legs, took a breath, and jumped. For a harrowing second he hung suspended in the air. Suddenly the ground rushed up to meet him. He landed firmly on both feet but the slippery slope proved more treacherous than he had counted on. His legs swept out from under him. The next thing he knew, he was hurtling down the bluff, out of control and unable to stop.

Clay thought of the boulders ahead and tensed. If he should smash into them going that fast, he'd break half the bones in his body. He threw out his free hand and clutched at the ground but it was like clutching at a sheet of cold grease. He could find no purchase. His momentum built. Everything around him became a confused jumble of streaking images.

In desperation Clay slammed both heels hard into the ground and laid flat on his back. He jammed both elbows into the earth. A cry was almost torn from his lips as skin was ripped from the back of his arms and upper thighs. In front of him loomed a boulder. He hurtled to one side and careened off it, suffering a jarring blow which snapped his teeth together. The collision also helped to slow him down.

Another boulder appeared. Clay lunged as he

shot close by it and caught hold with his left arm. The jolt of stopping about wrenched the arm from its socket. He clung on to catch his breath and allow the pain to subside.

Lightning pierced the murky veil overhead. The very next instant thunder seemed to vibrate the ground. The rain was a solid mass which beat at Clay's head and shoulders. And on top of all that, the wind roared without cease, pushing against him as might an invisible hand.

White Apache let go of the boulder. Rising into a crouch, he advanced, alert for others. Each step was a study in caution. He tested his footing before bearing down with his whole weight. In spots the earth had been transformed into slick mud. It clung to his soles, making the descent that much more dangerous.

For an eternity this went on. The boulders fell behind him and he came to a tract of rough ground. Ruts and cracks worn by erosion threatened to trip him. He had to stoop to see the ground and even then he could not see it clearly.

It seemed as if lightning rent the heavens every two or three seconds. Every bolt lit up the countryside, some brightly, others faintly. The thunder was continuous, some blasts close at hand, others farther off.

White Apache could barely hear himself think, let alone hear anything else. He nearly slipped in a rut and was able to stay on his feet only by falling into a crouch and using his left hand to support himself. It was hard to say for sure but he believed that he was close to the bottom. He looked around, seeking a particular cluster of weeds he had noticed before the storm began. Finding it would take a miracle.

The rain had flattened every weed and small bush in sight.

Suddenly another crackling bolt cleaved the firmament. In its brilliant but fleeting glare, White Apache was taken aback to spy a pair of troopers at the very limits of his vision. They were crouched on flat ground, their carbines tucked to their shoulders.

The glare died as quickly as it had flared. White Apache did not know whether they had spotted him, and he wasn't going to stay there to find out. Gliding to the right a score of feet, he hunched low to the ground and awaited the next close strike. He did not have to wait long. The bolt lit up everything around for a good 50 feet. And there, less than half that distance away, were two more soldiers.

It didn't take a genius to figure out that the troopers had moved in close to the bluff to keep him from slipping through their lines.

White Apache sank onto his belly and wormed his way further to the right. If he recollected correctly, there was a narrow wash on the east side of the bluff. A minute of hard crawling brought him to a low spine. Looping an arm over the top to pull himself up and over, he felt it sink into rushing water up to his wrist.

White Apache wriggled to the top and discovered the wash. Only where before it had been dry to the bone, now it held a torrent of runoff. He guessed it to be over two feet deep in the middle.

It gave White Apache an idea. He wedged the Colt into his holster, held the rifle aloft, and snaked down into the wash. Immediately the water enveloped him. A clammy sensation bathed his skin from the neck down. He barely had time to turn in the direction of the flow when he was hurtled along as if shot from a cannon.

In a twinkling White Apache was ten feet from where he had just been. He glimpsed the bottom sweeping toward him and spotted a pair of blue figures huddled to one side. Taking a breath, he ducked his head under. The next moment he flashed past them and they were none the wiser.

Jerking his head up, White Apache gulped in air. A grim smile touched his lips. He had done it! He had escaped the trap! Now all he had to do was survive the flash flood. He tried to veer to the right but the water resisted him. He flailed at the side but could not gain a handhold. When he attempted to dig his knees into the bottom to arrest his speed, he was nearly upended by the violent current.

Then the water swept around a bend. White Apache did not see it until too late. He flung out his left hand just as he hit. Somehow his arm acted as a lever and he was half-flipped, half-pushed, high up against the side. By sheer chance he found footing for his right leg and shoved off with all his strength. Like an ungainly bird, he flew over the top and sprawled onto his stomach in mud two-inches deep.

Swiftly White Apache shoved to his feet and lurched toward the nearest cover, which happened to be a wall of mesquite. Ducking under a limb, he squatted and took stock. The Colt was still in its holster and the Bowie was in its sheath. Both were splattered with mud, nothing a thorough cleaning couldn't take care of.

It would have been nice for him to be able to rest for even a short while, but White Apache knew better than to stay in one spot for very long. Once the storm ended, the cavalrymen would search the bluff from bottom to top. When they learned he wasn't there, they would fan out and search for him. He had to be long gone by then.

Weaving through the mesquite to an open space, White Apache faced in what he hoped was due east and broke into a shuffling run. Five strides later he halted, riveted by the sight of tethered horses off to the right. He had completely forgotten about the string in his haste to get away.

Slinking from cover to cover, White Apache moved toward them. It seemed unlikely that the officer in charge had neglected to post guards, yet he saw none. At the last bush he paused to be doubly certain.

The drenched mounts stood close to one another, their heads hung low, some of them quaking with every flash of light. They looked utterly miserable.

Not one lifted its head when White Apache darted over to them and went to untie a black gelding. He would never know what made him glance around. He just did, and saw rushing toward him an Apache warrior dressed in an Army uniform with a carbine held on high to bash him in the head. Instantly he brought up the Winchester to parry the blow. He succeeded, but it was so powerful that he was rocked on his heels and almost lost his grip on the rifle.

In a blur the scout struck again, aiming the stock at White Apache's midriff. White Apache pivoted. He was spared the brunt but was still nailed hard enough to rack his ribs with agony. Thrusting with the Winchester as if it were a spear, he drove the barrel into the warrior's side. The Apache doubled over. A short chop to the base of the skull was all it took to drop the scout where he stood.

Above the din of the storm a shot rang out. White

Apache spotted a big trooper hurrying toward him. Where there was one there were bound to be more, so rather than stand his ground, he wheeled, leaped astride the gelding, tore the reins free, and was off into the chaparral before the onrushing trooper could put a slug into him.

It was a grand feeling to be alive and racing like the wind with the rain lashing his face! White Apache whooped in triumph as the vegetation closed around him. Nothing could stop him now! he told himself.

As if in ominous forewarning of events to come, the heavens rocked to the most tremendous eruption of thunder yet.

Chapter Eight

The Bowdries and the gunman known as Vasco rode due north from Pasqual's cantina. Until the middle of the afternoon the Tennesseans kept to themselves, riding a dozen yards or so ahead of the man with the pearl-handled Colt.

Razor trotted along close to Clem, as was the mongrel's habit. Of the three Bowdries, Razor liked Clem's company best. At night the animal slept at Clem's side. During the day the beast's eyes often lingered on the Bowdrie in the coonskin cap, much as a fawning child will dote on its favorite parent.

The gunman observed the animal's affection but did give it a second thught. Vasco had little interest in anything the Bowdries did. The way he saw things, it was bad enough that his employer had saddled him with the job of being their nursemaid. He just wanted to get the job over with and part company.

Vasco did not much like working with others. He was a loner, and had been since the terrible war between the North and the South devastated his family and sent him homeless and moneyless off into the world to make ends meet as best he could. Like many a displaced Southerner, he had taken to living by the gun. To survive, he relied on his speed and his wits. And so far they had served him in good stead.

The sun was high in the sky when Clem Bowdrie abruptly wheeled the mule called Stonewall and rode back to fall into place beside Vasco. The gunman did not hide his annoyance. Pulling his hat brim lower, he said brusquely, "Is there something I can do for you, mister?"

"I thought we'd talk some," Clem declared.

"About what?"

"You."

Vasco glanced sharply at the tracker. "I don't take kindly to folks who pry."

Clem showed those even white teeth. "I'm not fixin' to poke my nose where it don't belong. I just figured that since we'll be ridin' together a spell, we should at least be a mite friendly." Clem paused. "I can't help but notice that accent of yours. You're from the deep South, just like us. Whereabouts?"

The gunman had half a mind to tell the tracker that it was none of Bowdrie's damn business. But the man did have a point. They'd be together for days, maybe weeks. Vasco figured he should at least try to get along—for the time being. "Kentucky."

"Oh?" Clem said, sounding inordinately pleased. "We're Tennessee born and bred ourselves. From Possum Hollow. Ever heard of it?"

"Don't reckon I ever have, no," Vasco said. He caught Clell studying them. When Clell realized it, the man quickly looked away as if he had been caught doing something he shouldn't be doing. Vasco didn't know what to make of it.

"No one ever has," Clem had gone on with a grin. "Only about thirty folks live there. Them, and six hogs owned by Old Man Anderson. Those critters pretty much have the run of the place."

If there was any one subject in which Vasco had no interest whatsoever, it had to be hogs. He made no comment.

"Me and my brothers outgrew the place. We decided we wanted to see something of the world, so we lit a shuck for Texas and been wanderin' ever since. Truth is, though," Clem stopped and gazed wistfully eastward, "there are times when I get powerful homesick. That ever happen to you?"

"No."

"Not ever?"

"No."

"You never miss the smell of sweet grass covered with mornin' dew? You never miss the sight of them blue hills shimmerin' in the haze? You never miss cornbread or dumplin's or biscuits smothered with sorghum molasses? Or the bayin' of hounds after a coon?"

This time when Vasco looked at Bowdrie, it was in amazement. Vivid memories long buried welled up within him. For a few moments he was back in Kentucky, a young boy again, heading home after a day of hunting, a squirrel rifle over his shoulders, a powerful hankering for his ma's tasty grits quickening his steps. "I suppose I do now and then," he allowed softly.

"Ever think of goin' back?"

Vasco was sorry he had let the man start flapping his lips. He didn't enjoy dredging up his past. It hurt too much. "That part of my life is done and over with. I don't care to talk about it, if you don't mind. And even if you do."

Clem acted startled. "I'm awful sorry. I didn't mean to upset you."

For several minutes they went on without speaking. Vasco hoped the man in the baggy buckskins would take the hint and leave him be, but he had no such luck. Out of the blue, Bowdrie made a remark which shocked him.

"I'll bet your ma was a true lady. She probably cottoned to fancy dresses and made you wear shoes even in the summer."

"How in the world did you know that?"

Clem laughed lightly. "I'll also bet she made sure you never missed a day of schoolin'."

Vasco looked at the tracker for the third time, but this time he saw things he had not seen before. Such as the lively, intelligent gleam in the other's deep blue eyes. And such as the genuine friendliness mirrored by the other's surprisingly smooth features. "What are you? One of those mind readers I heard tell about?"

"Goodness gracious, no." Clem clucked at the mule when Stonewall slowed. "A body can tell a lot about a person from the way they talk and act and dress. Take you, for instance. You talk real proper-like, just like those who have a lot of book learnin'. And you keep your clothes all neat, your boots rubbed to a shine. Just like a person whose ma was fussy about such things."

The gunman felt a newfound respect for the talkative Tennessean. "You have me pegged," he confessed. "You're downright incredible."

Bowdrie's cheeks tinged crimson. "Shucks, I'm no great shakes, mister. I never had me any schoolin'. Pa claimed it was a waste of time. He wouldn't abide a book in our cabin." Clem's mouth pinched together. "Ma could read and write some, and she taught us a little on the sly. Enough for my brothers and me to scrawl our names when we need to."

"Where are your parents now? Back in Possom Hollow?"

"I wish. No, Pa died a few years after the war. He couldn't stand what had happened to the South. It plumb broke his heart." Clem took a breath. "As for ma, she didn't much care to live once pa went to his reward. She wasted away to nothin'."

"I'm sorry to hear that," Vasco said, and meant it. The War had played hell with so many lives, his own included.

Clem shrugged. "Like you said. That part of our life is done and over with. We have to get on with livin' or we'll just brood ourselves into an early grave."

"Anyone ever tell you that you have a way with words?" Vasco asked innocently, and was puzzled when the tracker blushed again. The man couldn't take a compliment if his life depended on it.

At that juncture Clell Bowdrie joined them, looping back alongside Clem, who shot him a stern glance. "Don't mind me. Since you two are bein' so friendly, I thought it proper I should be, too." He nodded at Vasco. "It ain't every day Clem takes a shine to someone."

The gunman saw no reason for the brother to make an issue of it. He was about to say something to that effect when Tick Bowdrie let out with a short piercing whistle which sounded exactly like the cry of a hawk. The signal caused the other Bowdries to face front and grip their rifles.

Ahead of them lay a wide canyon. To the west grew willows and alamos. Vasco knew that neither grew far from water, so he suspected there must be a spring or a tank hidden among the trees.

But it wasn't the island of green or the likelihood of water which had prompted Tick Bowdrie to whistle. He reined up to wait for them, then announced, "I spotted some Injuns about the same time they spotted me. Five or six, maybe more. They ducked back into the brush."

"Apaches?" Vasco asked.

"I couldn't rightly tell. They moved too blamed fast."

Clem moved into the lead. "Let's go have a look-see. Maybe they'll parley. If they're Apaches, they might know where Taggart and the renegades hide out. If they're not Apache, they still might have seen some sign of him. It won't hurt to ask."

"Apaches ain't the only hostiles hereabouts," Clell noted. "We'd best be rememberin' that."

Vasco scanned the dense vegetation as they warily approached. He was impressed by the Bowdries. They had spread out about ten feet apart and held their rifles loosely across their thighs, ready for anything. Clem already had the Sharps cocked.

Sixty yards out, the Tennesseans reined up. "This is as close as we go until they show themselves," Clell declared for the gunman's benefit. "It wouldn't do to ride on in there and end up lookin' like porcupines."

"They're watchin' us. I just know it," Tick Bowdrie said.

Vasco felt the same. It made his skin itch as if from a heat rash. He would never let on, but he fought shy of tangling with Indians whenever he could. They were too unpredictable, for one thing.

For another, they liked to mutilate their enemies, and Vasco had a secret dread in that regard.

Suddenly Razor growled and took a few steps but stopped at a word from Clem.

A warrior had appeared at the tree line. He was taller than most Indians Vasco had seen, and stark naked. Arms held out from his sides to show he meant no harm, the man came toward them. His black hair hung in a wide bang at the front and thin strands behind. Paint had been smeared on his face. Decorating his body were several tattoos.

"Look at this yack, prancin' around in the altogether," Tick muttered. "And I heard a Yankee once claim that Injuns are just like ordinary folks!"

Clell chortled. "Maybe you shouldn't look, Clem," he joked. "Ma used to say it's downright sinful for a person to show so much skin."

The tall warrior halted 20 feet away. Tapping his chest, he said in passable Spanish, "*Estamos* amigos. No shoot us. We are friends."

Clem surprised Vasco by answering in the same language. "You are a Yuma."

"*Si*, senor. *Me llamo* Pelo."

The revelation disturbed Vasco. He had never had any dealings with the Yumas, but he had been told they were as two-faced as a politician. A man never knew from one day to the next what sort of reception the Yumas would give him. At times the tribe was on friendly terms with whites. At other times, and without prior warning, they would set on innocent travelers and viciously massacre them.

"You are part of a war party," Clem Bowdrie said.

Pelo smiled. "No. No. We are hunting. We look for deer. Need meat in village."

Vasco was suspicious. The Yumas lived along the Colorado River, many miles from the canyon. It was unlikely the band had traveled so far in the pursuit of game.

"He's lyin', Clem," Clell said in English. "They don't paint their faces to go huntin'. My guess is, they're lookin' for skin to lift."

By that, the Tennessean referred to the Yuma custom of not only scalping an enemy, but peeling off the skin of the entire head, including the ears.

Vasco saw Pelo's eyes dart toward the skinny tracker. He had a hunch the warrior spoke English, but would not admit as much. To test his idea, he interjected, "If he's lying to us, let's shoot him and be done with it."

The Yuma took a short step backward and nervously wet his lips. "Me friend," he stressed in Spanish, wagging his empty hands. "I not want hurt white men. You come. Much water. You drink with us."

Tick gazed toward the trees. "That reminds me. Where do y'all suppose the rest of them heathens got to? Not a one has showed himself except for our friend here. I don't like it much."

Neither did Vasco. It was obvious the Yumas were up to something or Pelo would not be acting as agitated as a caged bobcat. But for the life of him, Vasco could not guess their intent. An attack would be surefire suicide, since the warriors would be gunned down before they covered half the distance.

Vasco glanced toward the vegetation, seeking some sign of the warriors. As he did, Razor swung to the north and growled a low, menacing challenge. Before the gunman quite knew what was happening, all hell broke loose.

Pelo let out with a screech that would have raised the hackles on a corpse, even as he threw himself to the ground. To the north a dozen voices answered with cries every bit as strident, and up over the side of a gully which neither Vasco nor the Bowdries had realized was there charged the rest of the war party. About two-thirds were armed with mallet-headed clubs and round hide shields. The rest carried long bows and had shafts notched to sinew strings.

Vasco reacted without thinking. His right arm flashed to his Colt and the pistol leaped from its holster with lightning speed. Three times his thumb worked the hammer. Three shots sounded in swift succession, leaving a pair of Yumas dead before they could unleash their deadly arrows.

Clem's first shot was only a heartbeat less fast. The big Sharps boomed and the foremost warrior, a stocky specimen wildly swinging a war club, was cored through the brain by the heavy-caliber slug.

Tick and Clell also cut loose, the Spencer and Winchester banging like twin hammers.

An arrow whizzed past Vasco. He replied with the Colt. His horse uttered a piercing whinny, then pranced to one side. Swiveling, he saw Pelo leap up and spring at Clem. The tracker went to slam the Sharps into the warrior's brow but a blur of hair and sinew was on the Yuma first.

Razor tore into the warrior like a saw into wood. Teeth which could break bone ripped through soft flesh as if it were so much soggy paper. Pelo screamed as he was borne to the ground. He tried to fight back. He pushed and punched and kicked at the mongrel but he might as well have been flailing at a grizzly for all the good it did him. Razor's fangs sank in deep again and again. Blood spurted everywhere. Pelo's scream rose to a wavering crescendo. Then the wolf dog's jaws clamped on the tall warrior's throat and the scream abruptly died.

Vasco did not get to see what happened after that. A brawny Yuma swinging a war club was on him. He felt the heavy head smash against his left side and nearly cried out. His arm and leg went numb. Twisting, he pointed the Colt. The Yuma closed in again just as he fired.

Suddenly the gunman's horse buckled. Vasco threw himself clear to keep from being pinned but his numb limbs impeded him. He fell short. Before he could roll into the clear, his horse came down on his legs.

The pain was bad enough. Being caught fast was worse. Vasco jerked around and saw another warrior almost on him. The warrior's face was lit with bloodthirsty glee. Evidently the Yuma thought it would be an easy kill. Vasco disillusioned him with a shot to the sternum which spun the Yuma around.

The warrior staggered back, grit his teeth, and came at the gunfighter again.

Vasco had the Yuma dead to rights. Even though his legs were pinned, all he had to do was extend the Colt, pull back the hammer, and stroke the trigger. Which he did. But in the heat of battle he had forgotten to count his shots. When he squeezed, all he heard was a faint click as the hammer fell on an empty chamber.

Whipping the war club on high for a killing stroke, the stricken Yuma took a bound and was poised to swing when a buckskin-clad figure hurtled out of nowhere and rammed into him. The warrior was knocked onto his side. He tried to rise but Clem Bowdrie's revolver spat smoke and lead three times.

Behind Bowdrie yet another Yuma appeared.

"Look out!" Vasco shouted, to no avail. Clem could not hear him above the sudden thunder of Clell's and Tick's guns.

Bending to the left, Vasco got his hands on the stock of his Winchester and yanked the .44-40 from the boot. In a smooth motion he straightened, levered a round, and fired at the exact instant the warrior was about to plunge a knife into Clem's back.

The bullet caught the warrior low in the chin, passed completely through his head, and burst out above his ear. The man died on his feet.

At the very last moment, Clem had awakened to the danger and whirled. On seeing the Yuma crumple, Clem glanced at Vasco and smiled. "I'm obliged."

Vasco shifted, surprised he had been able to hear Clem speak above the din. Only then did he realize how quiet it had suddenly become. As he turned, he learned why. The battle was over.

Eight Yumas lay on the ground, two of them twitching as if having fits. Four others were in full flight to the northwest, and one was wounded. He hobbled along like an ungainly jackrabbit.

Tick and Clell were both still on their horses. A wide gash on Tick's left cheek showed how close a club had come to taking his head off. Clell, on the other hand, had an arrow sticking out of the fleshy part of his upper arm. It did not seem to bother him much.

Razor was astride Pelo, chewing hungrily.

"If they think we'll let 'em skedaddle, they've got another think comin'," Tick Bowdrie roughly declared. Bringing up his Spencer, he adjusted the sights and fired at a range of 40 yards. The last Yuma's arms flapped outward and for a second it appeared as if he were trying to sail into the air.

Instead, he plowed face-first into the ground.

Clell walked over to Razor, pointed at the fleeing warriors, and barked, "Fetch 'em."

The wolf dog was off like a shot, streaming low to the ground. One of the warriors looked back, saw it, and shrieked in mortal terror.

"I'd best lend a hand," Tick said, jabbing his heels into his mule.

"Wait for me!" Clell called. He went to lift the reins but the jutting shaft reminded him of his wound. Looking down in annoyance, he said, "Damn it all. I forgot about this toothpick. I reckon I should get it taken out before I do any more serious Injun fightin'."

"Climb down and I'll tend you," Clem proposed.

"First things first," Clell said. Kneeing his mount over to one of the twitching Yumas, he explained, "I don't want no blade between the shoulders while you're workin' on me." Slowly palming his Colt, he shot the warrior through the head. Then he moved to the next.

Clem, meanwhile, had bent to Vasco's dead horse and wedged both hands under the saddle. Grunting from the effort, the Tennessean tried to raise the saddle high enough for the gunman to slide out, but couldn't. Clem paused to catch a breath, saying so softly that Vasco barely heard, "Maybe ma was right all along."

"About what?" Vasco asked, not really paying much attention. He had been keeping an eye on the fleeing Yumas. Razor had already overtaken one and pulled the warrior to the ground. Tick was closing in on the last two and was in the act of unslinging his scattergun.

"Nothin'," Clem said much more bitterly than the circumstances warranted.

114

Vasco stared up at him as Clell's pistol cracked once more. The other Bowdrie came over, dismounted, and stepped to the dead horse, his left arm tucked to his side.

"Here. I can't use but one arm, but it should be enough."

It was. Ten seconds later Vasco was on his feet and rubbing his left leg to relieve a cramp. "Now it's my turn to be obliged," he told Clem.

The blast of a shotgun reduced the number of surviving Yumas by one. Tick rode on by the dead man at a leisurely pace while reloading the shotgun.

Clell was regarding the gunman closely. "That was some fancy shootin' you did, droppin' those first two before they could put arrows into us. If you hadn't been here, this would have turned out a whole lot differently."

Vasco hunkered and began to undo the cinch. "We'll have to head back to that saloon. Maybe I can buy a horse there. If not, we'll head for Fort Bowie. Sometimes the sutler has stock he sells."

"And lose at least two days, probably more?" Clell shook his head. "You heard your boss. We have a good chance of cuttin' the White Apache's trail if we hurry. We can't turn back." He held out his arm so Clem could inspect it. "You'll just have to ride double with one of us."

"With me," Clem volunteered.

Vasco was confounded by Clell's reaction. The stringbean stiffened and grabbed Clem's wrist and gave it a hard shake.

"Over my dead body! I've gone along with this because I figured you knew what you were doin'. But now I ain't so sure. Maybe you ought to wait until the Taggart business is done with."

"I'm all grown up and can do as I darn well please," Clem replied angrily.

Vasco stood. "Flip a coin if you want. I'll ride double with whoever wins." He chuckled at their antics. "There's no need to fight over who gets the honors. It's not all that important."

Clell continued to glare at Clem. "If you only knew," he said, and then again, lower, as if half to himself, "If you only knew."

Chapter Nine

Antonio the Jicarilla came awake with a start and snapped up off the ground. He would have risen clear to his feet if not for a huge hand which caught hold of his shoulder and held him in place.

"Whoa, there, chief! What's your rush?" Sgt. Shawn O'Grady was smiling. "Maybe you should lie there and take it easy a spell. You've got a knot on the back of your noggin the size of a hen's egg."

The scout took stock. He was seated on a blanket near the horses. The troopers were huddled around three separate campfires, some drinking coffee, some eating hardtack. Capt. Benteen saw that he had revived and came over.

"Nice to see you back in the world of the living. I was worried there for a while. You were out all night."

Antonio stared skyward and discovered it to be true. The sun was perched a full hand's width above

117

the eastern horizon. "White Apache?" he asked.

"Escaped, I'm afraid," the officer answered, squatting. "Col. Reynolds will likely string me up by my thumbs when he hears I had the traitor trapped and let him slip through my fingers. But I did the best I could. Taggart has more luck than most ten men I know."

"No luck," Antonio disagreed. "Him want to live. Him have strong will."

Benteen bent the tin cup he held to his lips and took a noisy sip. "Whatever you want to call it, the bastard is free to go on murdering and plundering. Now every time I hear of another of his raids, I'll blame myself for not ending his miserable life when I had the chance."

"We go after him?"

"What good would it do?" Benteen pointed at the damp ground. "The storm lasted for another hour after he high-tailed it out of here. His tracks were all washed away by the rain. We don't have a trail to follow."

Antonio chose his next words carefully. He knew how overly cautious the officer could be, and it was important that the soldiers come along. Because one way or the other, he was going after the White Apache. The man had done what no others had ever done before. The white-eye had bested him in combat. Even worse, White Apache had not finished him off, but for some reason had let him live. Now each and every day Antonio would feel the deep gnawing pang of his shame. Every day, that was, until he avenged himself. Only by slaying Clay Taggart could he erase his humiliation.

"We not need trail," Antonio said. "Him head for Chiricahua Mountains. We maybe catch if we hurry."

"I don't think so," Benteen hedged. "The men are worn out. The horses are tired. There have been casualties, and we have the wounded to think of."

Sgt. O'Grady endeared himself to the Jicarilla for all time by saying, "We could send the wounded and the bodies back with Cpl. Ralston, sir. The rest of us could take the best horses and head out after Taggart. Maybe it will be a wild goose chase, but at least we'll have tried."

Like the warrior, the noncom craved the White Apache's blood. But not for his own sake. O'Grady wanted to see that Clay Taggart paid for the deaths of the two troopers. No one killed a man under his care and got away with it.

Antonio did not know why the sergeant spoke in his behalf. It didn't matter. The important thing was that it gave the captain pause, and Antonio quickly added, "It make colonel happy. Him know you do all you could."

"True," Benteen said thoughtfully. How well he knew that Reynolds liked to see his men give their all, and then some, in the performance of their duties. His superior would be more kindly disposed toward him if he were to chase Taggart to the ends of the earth. It would also reflect in his favor in the report Reynolds submitted to Washington.

"What do I tell the men, sir?" Sgt. O'Grady asked.

"Tell Ralston to be ready to ride out within the hour. He is to head for the post by the shortest route and is not to engage any hostiles along the way." Benteen took another sip. "You, Sergeant, will pick ten of our most seasoned men. See that they receive double rations and extra ammunition. Once Ralston has started off, we'll head for the Chiricahuas and hope to hell we catch sight of the White Apache before he gets there."

Antonio was so happy that he smiled and grunted. "This good thing you do. You see."

"I hope to hell you're right," said Capt. Benteen.

The new day started much as the last one had ended. Only this time Vasco was riding double with Clell Bowdrie when Clem rode up next to them and started in on him.

"I plumb forgot to ask yesterday. What's your first name?"

Both the gunman and the scarecrow frowned.

Vasco was not in the best frame of mind. He did not like losing his horse, a dependable animal which he had owned for years and which had carried him all the way from Kentucky. He did not like having to leave his saddle and war bag behind, secreted under a pile of brush in the stand of willows and alamo trees. And he liked least of all having to ride double with a man he hardly knew and did not care for all that much.

Now, on top of everything, the Bowdrie in the coonskin cap was prying into his personal life again. The gunman fixed a flinty gaze on him and said, "My first name is Boone. I was born in July. July fourth, to be exact. I have two brothers and a sister and they live in the Cumberland Mountains. My favorite color is blue. And my favorite food is fried steak. Now if there's anything else you'd like to know, see me again in five or six years." He exhaled in annoyance. "Damn. You are about as nosy as some women I've met."

Clell burst out laughing.

"There was no call for you to be so rude," Clem declared, and smacked the mule hard to get it to pull ahead of them. Razor tagging along, Clem soon went around a bend in the game trail they were following up into the hills which bordered the Chiricahuas and was lost to sight.

"I didn't mean to get him riled up," Vasco mentioned. "But your brother does too much prying for his own good."

"That Clem sure is a caution," Clell agreed good-naturedly. He did not act at all upset. In fact, he seemed in a better mood than he had before the gunman spoke his mind. "Maybe Clem will take the hint now and quit pesterin' you."

"Is he like this with everyone he meets?"

The skinny Tennessean found that hilarious. When he stopped cackling, he said, "No. I can't rightly say Clem is. You're a special case." Clell twisted and nodded at the gunman's Colt. "Maybe it's that fancy shootin' iron of yours. Or the way you talk."

Vasco was at a loss to know what that had to do with anything. But he did recollect Clem saying that he had a nice way with words. "If you don't mind my saying so, your brother is more than a little peculiar. You'd better have a long talk with him or one of these days he'll ask someone the wrong question and be shot dead before he can explain himself."

"Oh, I wouldn't fret on that account," Clell said. "Clem don't usually take to strangers the way Clem has taken to you."

"Ain't that the truth," threw in Tick Bowdrie to their rear.

Vasco turned. The last brother was a few yards away, riding with the Spencer in the crook of an elbow. Adorning his belt were twelve new scalps, so fresh the undersides were speckled with dots of dry blood.

Tick realized they had drawn the gunman's in-

121

terest, and smirked. "I know what you're thinkin'. Why would any hombre in his right mind waltz around with a bunch of smelly scalps tied to his waist?" He patted them. "These are money in the bank, mister. The State of Sonora is payin' good coin bounty for Injun scalps. They're mainly after Apache hair, but they're not too fussy. An even dozen scalps will bring us a tidy little poke."

"So you're scalphunters as well as bounty killers," Vasco remarked.

"I don't know if I like your tone, mister," Tick responded. "You make it sound as if we're the scum of the earth, when the truth is that we go around doin' jobs that need doin' but which no one else will do. We've made wolf meat of killers, footpads, deserters and worse. Apaches, Comanches, Comancheros, you name 'em, we've licked 'em. And what thanks do we get? None at all. It's enough to give a man second thoughts about his line of work."

Vasco felt little sympathy for the Bowdries. No one forced them to do what they did. They had picked the path they were on and they had to live with the consequences. The same as he did. As anyone did.

"When you get right down to the chase, gunfighter," Tick had gone on, "we ain't much different than you are."

"How do you figure?"

"You hunt folks down for money, same as us. You kill them for money, same as us."

Vasco did not much like the comparison. "That's where you're wrong. I sell my gun to the highest bidder, sure, but all that buys is my protection. I don't go tracking people down like you do. I don't shoot folks in cold blood like you did those three deserters."

"So you heard about that, did you?" Tick said. "I should of known those Army no-accounts would go tellin' tales out of school. Well, it don't matter. We got the job done and that's all that counts."

"I disagree," Vasco said. "It's not getting it done but how you get it done which is important. A man has to have some principles to stand on or he isn't much of a man."

Clell Bowdrie snickered. "Listen to you! A gun-man with scruples! Now I've about heard everything."

Tick chimed in with, "Next thing you know, brother, we'll be hearin' of Apaches taken to preachin' the Good Book!"

Both brothers laughed. As much as Vasco resented their sarcasm, he held his peace. He told himself that he had a job to do. He reminded himself that his employer would not take very kindly to him gunning down the men he was supposed to work with. His personal feelings were not important.

And all the while, deep down inside, Boone Vasco wondered if perhaps there was a kernel of truth in what the Tennesseans had just said. So what if he was picky about the work he took? So what if he wouldn't turn bushwhacker or bounty killer? Was there really all that much of a difference between his way of life and that of the Bowdries? And if not, what should he do about it?

The rest of the day proved uneventful. The brothers kept pretty much to themselves and Vasco spent most of the time pondering. Twilight shrouded the Chiricahuas when they made camp in a ravine watered by a small spring. After the horses had been tended to, Vasco strolled off to be by himself. Among a cluster of boulders he took a seat and leaned back to roll himself a smoke. He took his sweet time, admiring the sky as it darkened to a sea blue and then to ink black. As he finished rolling, he heard footsteps. Someone halted near the boulders and sighed. Moments later more footsteps heralded a second party.

"Mind if we talk?" Clell Bowdrie asked.

"I have nothin' to say to you," Clem answered.

"I think you do."

Vasco had no intention of eavesdropping. He placed his boots flat and was about to stand when the scarecrow said the one thing that would glue him in place.

"You ain't been actin' like yourself since we hooked up with the gunfighter. Tick has noticed it, too. Something is stuck in your craw and you won't share it. Which ain't like you at all." Clell paused. "You've had your moody spells before, but nothin' like this. Why don't you come clean? We're family, ain't we? You know that we only want what is best for you."

"I want out."

A long silence ensued.

"Out how?" Clell inquired.

"Out of this rut of a life we're in. I'm tired of roamin' all over creation with no place to call home. I'd like to have a roof over my head and a stove and a bed and all them things that make a place special. Just like we had back in Possom Hollow."

"There's no goin' back. Nothin' is ever the same again."

"Who said anything about relivin' the past? I want to go forward, not back. I want us to make something of our lives. I want us to do more than go around killin' folks."

"Tick and me are happy with the way things are.

We're good at killin', ain't we? And pa always said a body should pick work they're good at."

Clem's sigh was like the fluttering of a trapped bird's wings. "Listen to yourself. All you think about any more is killin'. What happened to the boy I remember? The one who was goin' to be the best damn farmer in all of Kentucky?"

"He died when pa did. And he was buried when ma passed away. Havin' a farm was a pipedream, Clem. The foolish notion of a boy who spent too much time daydreamin'. Well, now I'm a grown man, and I've learned that this old world of ours ain't all that nice a place to live in. We have to take what we can from life, and the Devil take the hindmost."

"That's a hard way of seein' things, Clell. Awful hard. Ma and pa never saw life that way. They were fine, decent folks who always tried to do what was right."

"And look at what it got 'em," Clell declared with passion. "An early grave for both, with nothin' to show for all their sweat and tears but a farm which couldn't feed all of us proper in a good year—"

"They had us to show for their love and devotion," Clem interrupted.

Another strained silence followed. Vasco felt awkward listening but he could not bring himself to stand up and let them know he was there. They might not take kindly to it, and he wouldn't blame them. He figured it best for him to sit still until they were gone.

"I'm serious about callin' it quits," Clem stated. "I'm tired of this kind of life, tired of never knowin' from one day to the next whether I'll get a bullet in the back tomorrow. I'm tired of livin' out of saddlebags and spendin' half my time in a saddle. I want something more."

"You've got your heart set on this, have you?"

"More than you will ever know."

"Damn that gunfighter, then. He was the one who put the notion into your head. I saw it. Way back at the saloon, I saw it. So I'm not surprised. Just powerful disappointed that you'd let the likes of him break us up."

"It's not him so much as the life he's lived. It set me to thinkin', is all."

"Bull. I know better." Clell's voice began to fade. "Well, you do what you have to, and Tick and me will do what we have to. Just remember that whatever you decide, we're your kin and we'll always be your kin."

Vasco was confused. He could not understand how the life he had lived, as Clem put it, had persuaded the towheaded Bowdrie to change his ways. And he did not much like being blamed for the breakup of the brothers when he had done nothing to encourage it. He listened for the sound of footsteps and thought he heard Clem leave. After waiting a full five seconds to be certain the bounty killer would not spot him, he rose and stepped around the boulder.

A few yards away, seated on another, was Clem Bowdrie. The Tennessean had his face buried in his arms and was sniffling so quietly that Vasco could not hear him. The gunman stopped short, hoping the tracker wouldn't notice. But just then Clem looked up and saw him. "I'm sorry," Vasco blurted. "I didn't mean to intrude."

"Oh, Boone!" Clem cried, rising. "You must have heard us. What am I going to do?"

"What are you asking me for?" Vasco replied testily. "Why do you think so highly of me, anyway? What did I ever do to deserve it?"

Clem shuffled over, wiping a buckskin sleeve across eyes which streamed tears. "You don't know yet, do you? After all the hints I gave?"

"What the hell are you talking about?"

"Me. Us. How I feel about you."

"Now listen here, mister—" Vasco began, gesturing. He choked off when Clem sprang at him and he was hugged hard enough to bust his spine. "What the hell!" he roared, reaching up to shove Clem away. His hands pressed flush against the Tennessean's chest, and suddenly his whole world turned topsy-turvy.

Clem Bowdrie had breasts.

Clay Taggart could not believe the run of luck he was having with horses. It was the day after he had escaped the patrol's noose, about the middle of the afternoon, when the gelding he had stolen showed signs of going lame. And he still had a long way to go before he would reach the Chiricahuas.

Taggart halted to examine the horse carefully. One leg was slightly swollen. By his reckoning he could get another five or six hours out of the animal if he did not push too hard, so he forked leather and rode on at a brisk walk.

The storm system had long since passed him by and gone eastward. The last he had seen of it had been late the night before when the eastern horizon had been rent by lancing bolt after bolt.

White Apache was grateful for Nature's tantrum. Thanks to the heavy rain, the gelding's tracks had been obliterated. It would be impossible for the patrol to pick up his trail. He was safe, and in a few days he would be at Sweet Grass among the only friends he had in the world, Delgadito and the other renegades.

The ride gave Clay time to think. He mused on recent events and plotted the course of action he would take once he was reunited with the Chiricahuas. For several weeks now he had been toying with the notion of paying one of the men who had helped lynch him a special visit, and he decided that he had put it off long enough.

Clay was going to make every last one of the vigilantes suffer, just as he had suffered that terrible day when they had looped a rough rope around his neck and hung him from a handy limb. He could still recall in all too upsetting detail how it had felt to have that rope bite deep into his flesh, how horrifying it had been to have the life nearly strangled out of him. If not for Delgadito ordering that he be cut down, his life would have ended there in the Dragoons with no one ever being the wiser.

Miles Gillett would have gotten away with killing him. Gillett, who had already stolen the heart of the woman Clay had adored, would then have been able to legally steal Clay's land with impunity. As things had turned out, Gillett did get the land, but not without paying a heavy price, a price that would climb in the weeks and months ahead.

Clay wished he could have been at the Triangle G to see the rancher's face when Gillett woke up and saw the bull's head. He wondered how his bitter enemy had taken it. Knowing Gillett as he did, he was certain there would be retaliation of some sort.

Gillett never abided an insult, nor did he ever let anyone get the better of him. The man would not rest until he had paid Clay back.

Well, let him try! White Apache reflected. He relished their clash. Even though the odds were so high against him, even though he had lost everything worthwhile and had no chance to reclaim any of it, even though fighting on seemed to be pointless, that was exactly what he would do.

As Clay's pa had liked to say, there were two kinds of men in the world; quitters and doers.

Quitters always had a hundred and one excuses for not doing this or that. Quitters saw life in its darkest terms and regarded sunny days as simply lulls between storms. Quitters had the habit of saying "No!" so much that it was always the first word out of their mouth whenever anyone asked them to do something new.

Doers, on the other hand, were like ravenous wolves. They seized life by the throat and tore at it in great gulps, relishing every moment, making the most of each and every day. When a job had to be done, they went out and did it with no whining or groaning or complaining. Doers did, and that was that.

Clay Taggart was a doer. As a rancher he had worked hard every day from dawn until well past dusk to make his ranch a success. He always put all his energy into doing whatever had to be done. And it would be no different now. He had devoted himself, heart and soul, to taking revenge on Miles Gillett. Nothing short of his death would stop him.

Or so Clay vowed for the umpteenth time as he reined up shortly before sunset to make camp. The cavalry mount was holding up better than he had counted on. It should carry him through half the next day if he were careful.

Dismounting, Clay stretched, then stripped off the saddle and bridle. Both he draped over an egg-shaped boulder. He took the precaution of tethering the horse using a picket pin he had found in the saddlebags.

Supper was next on Clay's mind. He worked the lever of his Winchester and started off to find game. The prospect of rabbit stew appealed to him but there were not many rabbits to be found in that arid area. He stepped to the top of a knoll and happened to gaze westward. An oath burst from him.

Not a mile away, rising sluggishly into the cooling air, were tendrils of dust which shimmered in the fading sunlight. There could be little doubt. Whoever it was, they were after him.

Chapter Ten

It was getting dark much too fast to suit Antonio. The Jicarilla twisted in the saddle to regard the western sky. Almost all of the sun was gone. Long shadows were spreading across the land like living fingers, shrouding more and more terrain with every passing moment.

They were so close to their quarry, too. All they needed was another five minutes. Antonio was sure of it.

The scout could tell by the hoofprints they had been following since about noon that the White Apache's mount limped at times. It explained why the renegade had held the animal to so slow a pace. Taggart would have been smarter to forget the horse and continue on foot.

The warrior shifted to the right. The officer was also studying the sun, a sure sign that Benteen was giving serious thought to calling a halt for the day.

Antonio did not want them to stop yet, so he said, "We close, Captain. Very close."

Oliver Benteen glanced at the tracks. He was not a skilled tracker, but even he could see that they were fresh. Although he had been about to call a halt, he elected to push on for another mile or so.

The officer rose in the stirrups to see above stands of manzanita which lay ahead of them. He saw the stark Chiricahua Mountains in the distance. Much closer rose a solitary knoll. From its crown they would enjoy a panoramic vista of the countryside and might catch sight of Taggart.

Goading his horse to greater speed, Capt. Benteen pulled abreast of the scout and said, "Make for that knoll. It's the highest spot around."

Antonio nodded. He did not bother to mention that he had seen the knoll from a long way back and had been making toward it the whole time. White men, he had learned, always liked to think that the best ideas were their own even when someone else merited the credit.

A growth of shindagger agaves forced the troopers to bear to the left to skirt the obstacle. For a brief span they could not see the knoll. Then they emerged onto an open belt which would take them to the knoll's base, and Capt. Benteen promptly gave the command which brought the cavalrymen to a gallop.

Antonio did not like to rush forward so recklessly, but he did not speak up. Another thing he had learned about white men was that officers were very temperamental about having their orders questioned, even when those orders were liable to get them killed.

The Jicarilla was not the only one who was bothered by the command. Sgt. Shawn O'Grady found it harder to stay close to the officer. He had made it a point to do so every step of the way. The captain had been wounded once; O'Grady was not going to let the officer be hurt a second time. So it was that when the noncom spotted the dull glint of metal at the top of the knoll, he immediately veered toward Benteen to cut his superior off and put his own body between the officer's and their goal.

Up on the crown, Clay Taggart had the front bead of the Winchester centered on the officer's chest, the hammer cocked, and his finger on the trigger. Once he killed the captain, he knew the others would see fit to call off the chase. Taking a quick breath to steady his aim, he fired.

At the very instant the .44-40 boomed, Clay saw the big noncom fill his sights. The slug struck the trooper high in the sternum and hurled him from his onrushing mount as if he had been walloped by a blacksmith's heavy hammer. The rest of the patrol slowed, some of them milling in confusion.

Clay fed another round into the chamber and tried to fix another bead on the captain. The prancing horses and growing darkness thwarted him. He snapped off a shot but hit a private instead. The soldier clutched at his shoulder yet stayed in the saddle. Then the bunch of them broke for the manzanita, some to the right, some to the left.

Their Apache scout opened fire, blasting away three times, firing on the fly but firing so accurately that Clay had to duck down as the bullets whined off the rock close to him. He brought up the Winchester again, too late. The scout gained cover.

Clay glimpsed some of the troopers hurriedly dismounting. The officer had gone to the left so he concentrated on the brush there, hoping the man would recklessly expose himself.

Capt. Benteen was not about to do so. Crouched low under a manzanita, he stared out at the prone body of Sgt. O'Grady. Benteen knew that the noncom had sacrificed himself on his behalf. It shook Benteen to the core of his being. He had been rash, and that rashness had cost the life of a good man.

Tearing his gaze from the pool of blood forming under O'Grady, Benteen saw four of his men and the scout 30 yards off. He motioned for them to keep down and one of the privates nodded.

Trooper Decker scrambled up behind the officer. "Are you all right, sir?" he asked in genuine concern.

"Fine," Benteen said. Five other soldiers were close by, including the one who had been shot in the shoulder. Benteen crawled on his hands and knees to them. "How is it, son?"

"I'll make it, sir," Pvt. Simmons said through partially clenched teeth. Another trooper was carefully prying his shirt back to expose the bullet hole. Simmons had been fortunate. The slug had penetrated just under the collar bone and exited above the shoulder blade, sparing his vital organs and major veins.

"What do we do, Captain?" inquired another man. "Sneak up on that son of a bitch?"

Benteen faced the knoll. Night was almost upon them, and there would be no moon. Despite that, they would be hard-put to reach the knoll without being detected. The White Apache had the advantage. And Benteen would be damned if he was going to lose another man if he could help it. "No. We'll lay low here for a while, then withdraw when I deem it safe. Simmons will have to be taken care of, and for that we'll need a fire." He paused to look at O'Grady one more time. "We'll wait to attack until daylight."

"Whatever you say, sir," Pvt. Decker said, "but I wish you'd reconsider. We all liked Sarge a lot. We should make that lousy traitor pay. Just say the word."

It was tempting. Oh so tempting! But Capt. Benteen shook his head. "One dead man is quite enough, thank you. Mark my words, though. If we ever get our hands on Clay Taggart, he'll regret the day he was born."

At that very moment the object of their hatred and wrath was climbing onto his horse. White Apache had saddled up right after noticing the dust cloud, then taken his position on the knoll. The leather creaked as he sank down, raised the reins, and tapped his legs against the animal's flanks.

Holding the gelding to a walk, he wound down the slope and off toward the hills which bordered the haunts of the Chiricahuas. They were so close that he had the illusion he could almost reach out and touch them. Once there, he believed he could relax. Few patrols ever ventured very far into the vast Apache stronghold.

It would not have been hard for White Apache to have picked off more of the troopers. Other than the scout, none were his equal at woodlore. He could have worked his way around through the brush and slain them quietly, using his knife or his bare hands.

Any of the other renegades would have done so. Fiero, Ponce, Cuchillo Negro and Delgadito would never pass up an opportunity to kill their despised enemies.

In that respect White Apache differed from the

warriors. His hatred was reserved for Miles Gillett and the posse Gillett had sent to lynch him.

As for the lawmen and soldiers throughout the territory who were on the lookout for him, and as for the countless Arizonans who loathed his guts on general principle, Clay felt only mild resentment. They were not to blame for how they felt. Each and every one was an unwitting pawn in Miles Gillett's grand scheme. They had all been manipulated by Gillett into thinking that Clay was a traitor against his own kind.

The soldiers on his trail now were merely doing their job. Clay had fought them because they had left him no choice. If they had left him alone, no one would have died. He would have been content to go on to Sweet Grass unhindered.

But the days when Clay could roam the territory as he pleased were long gone. He had been branded a renegade. In the eyes of everyone else in the Territory he was a bloodthirsty butcher, and the whites would not rest until he was six feet under.

If he had any sense, Clay told himself, he would forget Miles Gillett, forget about getting revenge, and light a shuck for parts unknown. It was not too late. In Montana Territory or Wyoming Territory or maybe out in California he could change his name and begin life anew. He could grow a beard and mustache and change his appearance in other ways and no one would ever know his true identity.

But that would mean Miles Gillett went unpunished. That would mean Gillett got away with framing him for rape and stealing his land and having him strung up. That would mean Gillett lived to a ripe old age, with no one ever the wiser that he was one of the most despicable human beings on the face of the planet.

Clay could not allow that. He could not turn his back on everything Gillett had done and pretend it never happened. Miles Gillett's vile acts demanded that justice be carried out, and Clay was the only one able to carry it out. He would not fail.

Out of habit, Clay glanced back at the knoll. He did not expect the soldiers to come after him, so he was taken aback to see a figure on foot briefly silhouetted against the backdrop of sky. He caught only a glimpse, enough to distinguish the figure's long, flowing hair.

It was the Apache scout.

Clem Bowdrie found Boone Vasco seated on an earthen mound over a hundred yards from the campfire. He did not lift his head as she eased down beside him and primly folded her hands in her lap. "I've been lookin' all over for you since you pushed me away and ran off," she said softly.

Vasco said nothing.

"I'm sorry it came as such a shock. I reckon I should have come right out and told you."

Still the Kentuckian made no reply.

"My full name is Clementine. I'm the only girl in the family." She plucked at her baggy buckskin shirt and tweaked the corners of her mouth upward. "You're probably wonderin' about why I go around pretendin' to be a man. I'd like to explain if you'd let me."

When the gunman sat there with his head bowed, Clem took courage and hurried on. "I grew up a tomboy. It's my own fault, I suppose. I had to do everything my brothers did. I hunted with 'em, fished with 'em, went rompin' all over the mountains with 'em. It got so that I could hold my own against most any boy in the hills. Shootin', trackin', wrestlin', you name it, there wasn't a body who could lick me."

Clem peered at Vasco. The shadows hid his face and she could not tell if he were listening or not. She could not even tell if his eyes were open or closed. Swallowing, she forced herself to go on.

"It's not like I'm the only tomboy ever raised in Tennessee. Or Kentucky, for that matter. You must of knowed a few in your time, didn't you?" Clem paused to await an answer but there was none. Coughing, she said hastily, "So anyway, after our folks passed on, we struck out on our own. I saw no reason to change my ways. And since some people don't cotton to women who go around actin' like men, I took to wearin' these here baggy clothes so most wouldn't know. I wasn't tryin' to deceive anyone so much as I was tryin' to make my life a whole lot easier."

If Vasco was paying attention, he did not show it.

Clem's resolve wavered. She had made up her mind to tell him the whole truth in the hope that he would think more kindly of her. But it did not appear to be working.

"It never much mattered to me, bein' like a man and all. Not until I met you." Her voice lowered to just above a whisper. "I know I'm makin' a fool of myself sayin' this, but the moment I set eyes on you, I wanted you for my very own. I took to thinkin' about you every minute of the day and night. You were even in my dreams. About drove me loco."

At long last Boone Vasco stirred. He raised his head to stare at her but his eyes were still lost in the shadows.

Suddenly Clem could no longer contain herself. Her feelings gushed out in a flood of words. "If it helps any, I'm so, so sorry! I should have guessed that you wouldn't see me for what I am. I mean, I know that I'm awful plain. Plainer than most every woman I've ever met. Clell says that's why I can pass for a man so easy. Hardly anyone ever takes me for a woman." Forgetting herself, she put a hand on the gunman's arm. "I don't blame you for bein' put out with me. And I won't hold it against you if you never want to talk to me again. But at least say something. Let me know what you're thinkin'. It means more to me than I can ever say."

Vasco stared at her hand a moment, then lightly clasped her wrist and moved her arm aside.

"Oh? Is it that bad, then? You hate me?" Clem's shoulders sagged and she bit her lower lip. "I should have figured as much. A woman like me has no right to set her sights on a man like you. That's partly why I couldn't bring myself to come right out and tell you how I felt. I was afeared you'd laugh in my face. And who could blame you? I am ugly as sin. I—" She had opened her mouth to say more but froze when the gunman touched a finger to her lips.

"Enough, woman. You're worse than a damn biddy hen."

It had been years since anyone used that tone on Clementine Bowdrie and was able to get away with it. She averted her eyes, the tears pouring over her cheeks.

"I liked you better when you didn't jabber like one of those big city, highfalutin types," Vasco added gruffly.

Clem sniffled. "I'm sorry. I won't inflict myself on you again." Her legs nearly gave out as she tried to stand and she swayed and would have fallen had the man from Kentucky not caught her and sat her back down.

"Quit apologizing. You have nothing to be sorry for. If anything, I'm the one who should be begging your forgiveness."

"What?" Clem said, unsure whether her ears were working fine or whether they were stuffed up.

Boone Vasco held her hand in his and stroked her knuckles with a fingertip. "I had no call to get you this upset. My pa always told me that a true gentleman never makes a lady cry. I hope you'll see fit to overlook how I've been acting."

"I'd overlook anything you did," Clem declared without hesitation. She resisted an urge to pinch herself to see if she was imagining that the man she adored was actually holding her hand and speaking kindly to her.

"You've been honest with me. So it's only fair that I be the same with you," Vasco said. Standing, he began to pace, his thumbs hooked in his gunbelt. "This doesn't come easy to me. I'm not one of those jaspers who suffers from diarrhea of the jawbone."

Clem offered no comment. She was afraid that if she did, she would say the wrong thing and ruin the moment. This was the first time in her entire life that she had ever been drawn to a man, and it had her so befuddled that she knew she would make a total jackass of herself if she hadn't already.

Unknown to her, Boone Vasco was just as confused. At first he had been angry at her for tricking him the way she had done, but the more he thought about it, he came to see that she had not done it on purpose. And now, staring down into her tear-filled eyes, he became aware of another fact that troubled him so greatly he had to turn away or risk having her see the truth for herself, a truth he did not feel he was ready to share for fear that it would change his life forever.

Clearing his throat, Vasco began by saying, "I want you to know that I don't hold this mix-up against you. What happened, happened."

"Thank you," Clem said with more sincere gratitude than anyone had ever shown him in all the years he had lived.

Vasco had to clear his throat again. "But now that it's out in the open, there are a few things we need to settle." He paused. "For one thing, I'm not the marrying kind. There hasn't been a woman born who can throw her noose over me. I like the life I'm living and I have no hankering to change."

"That's not the idea you gave me before," Clem mentioned before she could stop herself. "It seemed to me that your life has been a lonely one."

"I don't know what gave you that hare-brained notion," Vasco declared, and wanted to kick himself for lying to her. "I like being able to do as I please, when I please. I like not having a woman to make demands on me."

"I'd never do that."

Truer words had never been spoken. Clementine Bowdrie was the most independent woman Boone Vasco had ever met. But he was not willing to admit as much, not when doing so would admit his own feelings. "Maybe so," he allowed, "but that doesn't change the fact you're grazing off your pasture. If you keep on like this, you'll just make yourself more upset. I'm not looking to get hitched."

Clementine had not made any mention of marriage. She had not thought that far ahead. All she asked was to be able to show him that there was more to her than a man might suspect at first glance. She wanted to hold him, to press her lips to his. And since she had always been a person who suited her actions to her thoughts, she began to rise to do just that.

But at that exact moment, not all that far to the north, gunfire erupted.

"Listen!" Vasco cried, swinging around. Secretly he was glad for the distraction. There had been a strange gleam in the woman's eyes, and for a moment he had dreaded that she was about to do something they would both regret.

From the camp came Clell's bellow. "Clem! Vasco! Where the hell are you two?"

"We'd better get back there," Vasco said. Without thinking he took her hand and headed for the fire. He had gone a third of the distance when he awoke to his mistake and let go of her as if her fingers were hot coals. "Sorry," he mumbled.

"No need to be."

Clell and Tick both had their rifles in hand and were gazing northward when their sister and the gunman stepped out of the ring of darkness. Clell scrutinized the pair and made as if to comment but apparently changed his mind.

Tick Bowdrie wagged his Spencer. "Sounded like a hell of a battle. My guess would be that those shots were no more than a mile off. We should go have us a look-see."

"In the dark?" Clell responded. "Who knows what kind of mess we might find ourselves in? Maybe some Apaches just wiped out a wagon train of pilgrims. Or maybe more Yumas are in the area." He gestured sharply. "I say we stay put until daylight."

Frowning, Tick turned to their sister. "What do you figure we should do, Clem?"

Clementine hesitated. Ordinarily she was the one who made their important decisions. Her brothers trusted her judgment, without question. Whatever she chose, they would do. But in this instance her mind was in too much of a whirl for her to think with a clear head. Her every thought was of Boone Vasco.

"Well?" Tick prompted.

"I don't rightly know," Clem admitted, all too aware of their eyes on her. She had never let them down before and it upset her to do so now. Acting on sheer impulse, she said, "If there are Apaches or Yumas that close, it would pay for us to find out before they swoop down on us. We'd better put out the fire and go see."

Tick sneered at his brother. "I knew I was right. Let's saddle up." He moved to the fire and doused it with the coffee. Smoke rose in lazy curls into the air where it was whisked away by the brisk breeze.

Boone Vasco thought they were making a mistake but he did not come out and say it. His employer had sent him to keep an eye on the trio. So where they went, he had to go. And, too, Vasco was so out of sorts over Clementine that he did as he always did when he was deeply disturbed; he withdrew inside of himself. He was hardly aware of helping to get the horses ready or of climbing on behind Clell.

The Bowdries moved out in single file, Tick in the lead. Razor hung back near Clem as was the wolf-dog's custom.

Quiet had claimed the night. The manzanita rustled from time to time, and once a coyote yipped.

Vasco knew he should have every sense alert. He shook his head to clear it but he could not stop thinking of Clem. His palms kept tingling as they had when he accidentally touched her chest. It provoked a hunger in him the likes of which he had not known since his late teens when he had been fond of a certain Kentucky mountain girl.

Their course took them up over a hill and down into a narrow canyon rimmed to the north by high walls of stone. Vasco had his Winchester across his lap but had his hand on the barrel, not the breech where it should be.

Suddenly Razor growled.

The Bowdries immediately reined up. Tick raised his Spencer and leaned forward over the saddle horn as if he had spotted something.

"What is it?" Clell whispered.

The answer came in the form of a ragged volley of gunfire from the brush directly in front of them.

Chapter Eleven

It was Pvt. Decker who brought the news to Captain Benteen.

"Sorry to bother you, sir, but I figured you'd want to know. We can't find hide nor hair of that Injun, Antonio."

The troopers had retreated under cover of dense brush to a clearing where the wounded soldier, Simmons, was being tended. Several other men, among them Decker, had gone to collect their scattered horses and had returned just minutes ago.

Benteen stiffened on hearing the report, and stood. "Could it be that he took a bullet and no one noticed?"

"No, sir," the private said. "Most of us remember him not having a scratch. The last anyone saw, he was hanging back by himself when we headed here."

"Then where—" Benteen began, and divined the

answer in a flash. "Damn him. He went after the White Apache by himself."

"Really, sir?" Decker said, grinning. "Well, that works out real nice, doesn't it? I mean, who cares if two Injuns kill each other off?"

Benteen's spine stiffened even more. "That Indian, Private, is a member of this patrol and a fellow member of the United States Fifth Cavalry. In my presence you will accord him the respect he deserves. Do I make myself clear?"

Decker went as rigid as a board, his hands at his sides. "Yes, sir!" he said crisply. "No offense meant, sir."

"It's a wise man who learns to control his tongue," Benteen stated. Striding to the small fire, he stared down at the wounded trooper a few moments. "We'll leave two men here to watch Simmons. The rest of us will mount up and go after Antonio. With any luck we can catch him before he gets himself killed."

While the officer was legitimately worried about the Jicarilla's welfare, Benteen had an ulterior motive which he shared with no one. In their pursuit of Clay Taggart, the patrol had traveled deeper into the wilderness than he had ever been before, into an area few white men ever visited. They were so far off the beaten path that he would have a hard time leading them back out again. It would be best if they had the services of someone who knew his way around.

Within three minutes the eight men were mounted and trotting eastward. Benteen had the troopers advance with their carbines at the ready. They moved as quietly as they could, which was still much too noisy to suit him. What with the rattle of their accoutrements and the creak of saddles, they made enough noise to be heard hundreds of feet off. But it could not be helped.

Presently Benteen spied the knoll. He swung to the right and came at it from the south. As expected, there was no sign of either Taggart or Antonio. He went on, slower than before, his pistol clutched in his right hand. The night was so dark that he could not see farther than a stone's throw away.

They entered a narrow canyon flanked by high cliffs to the north. Benteen stayed on the south side where manzanitas and other plant growth afforded ample cover. Having already lost three men too many, he was taking no chances.

Benteen could not say how far he had gone when he reined up to listen. Moments later he heard a sound that caught his breath in his throat. To the south a hoof had clumped against stone. Bending an ear in that direction, he heard another hoof fall. Someone was moving slowly toward them.

By pumping his right arm, Benteen signalled to his men to dismount. They clustered around him for their whispered orders. "Spread out at five-foot intervals. Don't fire unless I do."

"Is it Apaches, sir?" one of the troopers nervously asked.

"I don't know," Benteen said, "but who else would be out in this godforsaken country in the dead of night?" Again he motioned and they fanned out as he had directed. Turning into the brush, he crept all of ten feet, to where he could see a winding approach into the canyon from the south.

No sooner was Benteen in place than a rider materialized out of the murky veil of night. The man's features were next to impossible for Benteen to make out. Not so the buckskins that the man wore.

It couldn't be Antonio, the officer reasoned, since the scout had on an Army uniform. On several occasions Benteen had seen Apaches in buckskins, so to his way of thinking, that suggested the rider must be one. And since the White Apache was in that area, it stood to reason that the rest of the renegades were as well. Benteen's pulse speeded up as it occurred to him that the rider might be Delgadito himself.

Another rider appeared. Then one more. Benteen could scarcely contain his excitement. He had been given a heaven-sent chance to atone for his earlier mistakes. If he could bring down the renegades, it would go a long way toward making up for the loss of his sergeant and the other two men.

The officer glanced to the right. A row of pale faces were fixed on him. He faced the oncoming riders. The nearest was 40 feet out and closing. Benteen still could not distinguish the man's features. His every instinct screamed at him to open fire but he could not bring himself to squeeze the trigger until he was sure.

The matter was taken out of Benteen's hands when one of his men stepped on a twig which cracked loudly. Benteen saw the foremost rider lean forward and start to raise a rifle. Acting on the spur of the moment, out of fear for the safety of his men and in the belief that the rider was about to shoot, he opened fire.

At the blast of the pistol the troopers let loose with a volley from their carbines. None of them were skilled marksmen, however. In their haste and in the dark each and every one missed.

Tick Bowdrie lived through the initial lead hailstorm. Thinking that he had been fired on by Yumas or Apaches, and with no cover handy, he did that which his attackers were least likely to expect. Tick leveled the Spencer and charged, shooting at gun flashes. His mule pounded on down the slope into the thick of the brush. To his left a figure was framed by a manzanita and Tick instantly sent a slug into the man's torso.

Another volley rang out, so loud it was like the peal of cannons. Men were firing every which way. Tick's mule brayed and barreled into the growth. It took Tick unawares and before he could clamp his legs or grip the reins securely a low limb caught him flush across the chest, spilling him to the hard ground, where he lay dazed.

Meanwhile, Clell, Clem and Boone Vasco had taken cover. The gunman saw the brother and sister dart forward to aid Tick, drawing a flurry of rifle fire from the manzanita. Whipping the Winchester to his shoulder, he covered them, using muzzle flashes to guide his aim. Lead ricocheted off the boulders around him, some so close that one nicked his hat.

Vasco saw Clem suddenly go down and a lump leaped into his throat. Furiously working the lever of his rifle, he rushed to her side. The Winchester went empty as he sank to one knee to find she was unhurt, merely reloading the Sharps. She smiled at him, then burst from concealment to rejoin Clell.

Leaning against the boulder which had screened her, Vasco took several deep breaths. He had to get a grip on himself! he realized. Another careless act like that could cost him his life.

In the manzanitas, Capt. Oliver Benteen was on his knees, feeding cartridges into his pistol with hands which shook so badly he could hardly hold them. The Indians were attacking but his men were putting up stiff resistance, and at that moment he was prouder of them than he had ever been.

Inserting the last of the cartridges, Benteen slapped the hinge shut and rose. Two figures in buckskins had tried to rush the patrol and had been driven to ground. The pair were exchanging random shots with his soldiers. But he was more concerned about the one who had plowed into the manzanitas. For all he knew, the savage might still be alive, might be picking his men off one by one.

Benteen stalked through the underbrush, pausing every few steps to scour the shrublike trees around him. He glimpsed something move off to the left, something big, so he slanted toward it, the hammer of his Colt at full cock.

Not ten feet away Tick Bowdrie rolled onto his side and put his hands under him to rise. He froze on beholding a two-legged form skulking through the dark. The Spencer had been sent flying when he tumbled but he still had the shotgun slung over his back. He quickly unslung it, cocked the piece, and inched into a crouch.

Tick strained to see the bushwhacker. He could tell the man wore a dark shirt and pants and a hat. Beyond that, he had no notion whether the rifleman was white or red. The man's clothes were not any help since many Indians liked to wear white man's apparel and many frontiersmen went around in Indian garb.

Only one fact had any bearing for Tick Bowdrie; the man had tried to kill him. That earned the bushwhacker a one-way ticket to Hell, in Tick's book. He quietly rested the muzzle of the shotgun on a branch, aligned the barrel right where he wanted it, and waited for the man to take just one more step.

Capt. Benteen paused. A feeling had come over

him that he was in dire peril. He looked to the right and the left but saw no cause for alarm. Bending at the knees, he paid particular attention to those inky patches nearest him. Still he failed to see anyone.

The officer continued onward. Suddenly his mind registered the vaguest of human outlines. There seemed to be a man crouched behind a wide manzanita not three yards from him. Although he was uncertain whether his eyes were playing tricks on him, he didn't stand there waiting to find out. He dived, and as he did, a gun went off.

Tick Bowdrie knew he had missed. He also knew the bushwhacker had his position pinpointed. So as he fired, he leaped to the right, landing on his side in dry weeds. Crawling forward, Tick flattened next to a bush. He reached for the bandoleer criss-crossing his chest for another shotgun shell.

About that time, Trooper Decker came crashing through the undergrowth. The private had seen the muzzle blast of the shotgun light up the night and had caught sight of his superior apparently falling to the ground. Levering a round into his carbine, he raced to help the officer.

Tick spotted him. The Tennessean's fingers flew. In a blur he shoved in the new shell and brought the shotgun up. There was no need to aim. Not at that range. Not when using buckshot. He simply pointed at the center of his target, then fired. The figure seemed to blow apart from the waist up, and what was left crumpled like so much broken furniture.

Capt. Benteen had heard the crackle of limbs as someone sprinted toward him. He had suspected it was one of his men and opened his mouth to shout a warning. The thunderous retort of the shotgun came a fraction of an instant sooner. In sheer horror he saw parts of the trooper go flying every which way. Sticky drops of gore splattered his cheeks and neck.

The officer caught sight of the Indian. Sparked by blinding rage, he jumped erect and charged, working the hammer of his pistol as he did. His second shot jerked the savage around, but the man thrust up onto his knees and tried to elevate his gun. Benteen fired again, and again, emptying the revolver. At the last shot the killer pitched face down.

Benteen stopped, his rage fading as abruptly as it had flared. Behind him something pattered. For some strange reason it bought to mind the sound a dog made when frolicking in a field. He whirled, hoping he would have time to reload before whatever it was reached him. But he was only halfway around when a hurtling mass of sinew and fur rammed into him with the force of a grizzly bear. Long, tapered teeth flashed before Benteen's eyes. He could not help screaming when his shoulder was torn open clear down to the bone. In a panic he clubbed at the creature with his pistol but it did no good. The creature's fangs sheared into him again.

Capt. Oliver Benteen did not want to show weakness in front of his men. He had always taken pride in being as tough as the next man. Yet the onslaught of pounding pain was so intense that he could not keep from throwing back his head and screaming his lungs out.

In hindsight, it had been a mistake for Benteen to go after the White Apache. In hindsight, it would have been better if Benteen had left Antonio to fend for himself. And, in the fleeting instant of hindsight Benteen had before the beast's iron jaws slashed into his exposed throat, it would have been better if he had not screamed.

Clell Bowdrie heard that strangled cry and smiled to himself as he snapped off four shots from his Winchester to keep their attackers pinned down. Rising up, he sprinted into the vegetation. Once he was under cover, he set down the rifle and hastily unslung his Cherokee bow. Stealth was called for now. In that regard, the bow was preferable to the .44-40.

Quickly notching an arrow, Clell spied a pair of dark forms gliding toward him. He smoothly drew the sinew string back to his cheek, sighted down the shaft, centered the barbed tip on the figure's chest, and loosed the arrow simply by relaxing his fingers.

There was a loud thump and a louder grunt. The attacker staggered back, grasped at the feathered end of the shaft, then did a slow spin to the ground.

The other figure, panicking, commenced shooting wildly, swinging from side to side.

Clell kept on smiling as he pulled another arrow from his quiver and notched it. None of the shots were coming anywhere near him. Yet, at the same time, they let him know exactly where to aim. In another moment he was ready, his fingers beginning to ease off the nock, when a third dark shape dashed forward from an entirely different direction.

The lean Tennessean did not know if the newcomer had spotted him. It did not occur to him until seconds later that if he had stayed still, if he had not done anything to draw attention to himself, the man might have gone on by without noticing him. Instead, Clell swiveled and let the arrow fly. He acted hastily, without taking the moment or two needed to verify there were no trees or brush between the target and himself.

Clell's movement caused the figure to whirl. The arrow, flying true, was an arm's length from the bushwhacker when it struck a low manzanita limb and glanced upward, harmlessly deflected. Clell made a grab for a third shaft. But as he did, three shots shattered the chaparral and he was slammed onto his back.

The lean Tennessean could see stars sparkling far above. He attempted to stand but it was as if a tremendous weight had settled onto his chest. In addition, his limbs had turned to mush. He couldn't lift an arm off the ground, let alone raise his body. A warm, moist sensation spread over his chest and down across his belly. Clell wanted to call out, to yell to Tick and Clem to be careful, but even that simple achievement was denied him.

A black cloud enclosed Clell within an indigo cocoon. His final thought before the cloud consumed him was that he hoped his sister had found happiness at long last.

Unaware that both her brothers were dead, Clementine Bowdrie darted toward the undergrowth, the tail of her coonskin cap flying behind her. She had just fired the Sharps and resorted to her pistol. Someone took a shot at her so she responded in kind. Ducking under a leafy branch, she froze.

The night had gone strangely quiet all of a sudden. Clem listened but heard only the sigh of the wind. Tick and Clell were out there somewhere and she strained to locate them.

Also out there were killers who would gun her down if she were not careful. She could not afford a single mistake.

Clem had lost track of Boone Vasco in all the confusion. The last she'd seen, he had been dogging her footsteps. Now he had disappeared. She gazed back up the rocky approach to the canyon, fearing he had been slain. The very thought made her heart beat faster, made her mouth go dry.

Never in her wildest dreams had Clementine ever expected to meet a man she would desire. Never in her most vulnerable moments had she figured that one day she would want a man to want her. She had always been content being as she was. She had always been whole in and of herself. It was the shock of all shocks to learn she was just like any other woman who had ever lived. Like her mother and her grandmother and her great-grandmother and every last female who had ever born the name of Bowdrie, in her heart of hearts she yearned for a husband and a family and maybe a nice place to call their very own. It was—

The rustle of a body through the chaparral reminded Clem that this was not the time to be pondering her fate. It rattled her to think that she would let down her guard at that most crucial of moments. What was happening to her?

The rustle was repeated. Clementine extended her revolver even though she could see no one. Faintly to her ears came whispering. Shadows separated themselves from other shadows and flitted among the mazanitas. It seemed as if they were moving away from her but Clem did not move from her hiding place. Her intuition told her the time was not yet ripe. Then the shadows blended into the dark.

Again Clem sought some sign of the lean gunman from Kentucky but she was unable to see a trace of him. Her heart wrestled with her head. Part of her wanted to go back out among the boulders to find him. Another part of her warned that doing so was a virtual death wish. The bushwhackers were bound to spot her.

Which brought up an important point Clem had not considered until that moment. Who were their attackers? Her first thought had been that they were Injuns, but these men fought like no Injuns she had ever gone up against. Injuns made a lot of noise when they battled, whopping and hollering loud enough to raise the dead. These men fought without making a peep.

Minutes pregnant with tension dragged by. Fueled by her worry for Vasco, Clem grew impatient. She had not seen or heard anyone in quite some time. That might mean they'd had enough and gone elsewhere.

As fluidly as a she cat, Clementine stood and moved deeper into the vegetation. Her pa had shown her how to place her feet down loosely and lightly so that she did not make any noise. He had also taught her how to use terrain to her advantage. There wasn't an animal in Possum Hollow, wild or tame, that she couldn't sneak up on if she had half a mind to.

Injuns weren't animals, though. They were smarter than the smartest fox, deadlier than the biggest rattler. Combined with those traits was their uncanny wilderness savvy. As some of the old timers liked to say, Injuns had eyes in the backs of their heads and four ears instead of two.

Clem drew up short on seeing a body. Casting her eyes to both sides, she checked to see if enemies lurked in the vicinity before she stalked to the corpse to examine it. She expected to find a bronzed warrior. The sight of a cavalryman lying in a puddle of blood, his face contorted in a gruesome death mask, was such a jolt that she inadvertently gasped.

It couldn't be! Clem's mind shrieked. Setting down the Sharps, she ran her hand over the uniform, then inspected the face more closely. Sometimes Apaches and other Injuns dressed in the clothes of slain troopers. Yet there could be no doubt. This man was white.

A horrible thought intruded itself. Had they stumbled onto a cavalry patrol which had mistaken them for Injuns? The Army would not take kindly to having its own slain, no matter what the provocation. They were in a heap of trouble.

Stunned, Clem rose and moved on. Her thoughts were all scrambled and she could not decide what to do next. But her bewilderment was as nothing compared to that which she felt when she nearly tripped over another body and looked down at her feet to discover Clell's lifeless countenance staring back up at her.

"No!" Clem breathed, falling onto her knees by her brother's side. She took his hand in hers. "Please, no!"

Five pair of ears heard her outcry. Four of them belonged to the surviving soldiers who were a dozen yards to the north. As one, they wheeled and made for the sound, their carbines cocked.

The last pair of ears were those of Boone Vasco. The gunman had been desperately searching for Clem since losing sight of her when she dashed into the brush. Her cry was a beacon which drew him on the run. He knew that he should move quietly, but he didn't care. He wanted to reach her side.

The next second Vasco raced around a manzanita and came on Clementine bent over Clell's body. Her hands were clamped on his shirt and she was being racked by great sobs.

Simultaneously, beyond her, four men appeared. Vasco could see them clearly. He identified them as cavalrymen. He knew that a terrible mistake had been made and that he should not lift a finger against them.

But the quartet were bringing their carbines to bear on the distaff Bowdrie. It should have been obvious to them by her empty hands and the sound of her crying that she posed no threat to them. If they noticed, they took no heed. The muzzles of their guns leveled.

"Look out!" Vasco shouted, and let go of his Winchester. His right hand swooped to the nickel-plated Colt faster than he had ever drawn before or would likely ever draw again. It was a once in a lifetime draw, so perfect, so quick, that he had the gun out and had banged off two shots before his own brain realized he had done it.

Two of the troopers toppled but the other two opened fire, one of them at the gunman, the other at Clementine.

"No!" Vasco roared as he fired twice more, his shots so swift that they were like one. The soldiers fell, each cored through the head. Vasco stared, amazed at his own ability, and slowly started to straighten. Then he trembled as the blood in his veins changed to ice.

Clementine Bowdrie was sprawled across her brother.

Chapter Twelve

White Apache was nearing the north end of the canyon when the gunfire erupted. He did not know what to make of it. Nor did he have any time to mull over what it might mean. Seconds later, as he goaded the flagging roan up a short incline, the cavalry mount's bad leg gave out and the horse stopped dead in its tracks and would not go another foot. He slapped his moccasins against its sides. He whipped the reins. The animal refused to budge.

Sliding to the ground, White Apache turned. There had been no sign of the scout since that first glimpse, yet he was sure the warrior was still back there somewhere, and close.

White Apache darted into the manzanitas and crouched. It struck him that the useless horse might be of benefit after all. He could use it as bait. Flattening, he poked the barrel of the Winchester through the limbs so that it was trained on the animal, and waited.

The scout was bound to investigate. White Apache figured he might get at least one clear shot, which was all he needed.

Meanwhile the gunfire continued to rock the canyon, echoing off the cliffs to the north. It sounded as if a full-fledged battle were being fought.

Now that White Apache had a moment to think, a troubling prospect occurred to him. He reasoned that the patrol must be involved, and if the troopers had engaged enemies, those enemies had to be Indians. And since they were outside the boundary of the Chiricahua Reservation, the only Indians likely to be abroad in that region were renegades. Perhaps even his friends, Delgadito and the other members of the band.

White Apache wrestled with an urge to retrace his steps and go see. In doing so he might walk right into the scout's sights. It made more sense for him to dispose of the warrior first, then determine if Delgadito and the other Chiricahuas were involved. There was little he could do to help them, in any event. By the time he got there the battle was bound to be over.

The steady din of rifle and pistol shots made hearing anything else difficult. White Apache had to rely on his eyes more than his ears to locate the scout. He roved them from side to side, seeking any hint of movement. There would not be much warning. Apaches were like ghosts when they wanted to be.

It was then he noticed the wind had changed. That often happened at night, especially higher up in the mountains. Where before the breeze had been blowing from the northwest to the southeast, it now blew from east to west, carrying his scent back toward the knoll. Normally that would not matter. But some Apaches had such a keen sense of smell that they could sniff a man out if they were downwind of him.

White Apache shifted as an uneasy feeling took hold. He felt that he was being watched but he could see no one. He tried telling himself that his nerves were to blame, that the thought of the scout catching his scent had rattled him, but deep down he knew better. The Apache had found him.

Rolling quickly to the left, White Apache surged to his feet and ducked behind a bush. From there he circled wide to the south, stopping frequently to scour the chaparral. The Apache did not appear but he wasn't fooled. The warrior was waiting for just the right moment to strike.

It was unnerving to stalk through the shadowy manzanita, never knowing when the crack of a rifle might be the last sound he ever heard. A whisper of motion made White Apache bring up the Winchester but the scout did not materialize. Frustrated, he went on.

White Apache had no idea which tribe the warrior belonged to. Mescaleros, Jicarillas, White Mountain Apaches, Cibeques, and even Chiricahuas worked as scouts, a practice the Army encouraged since the day it had dawned on desk-bound commanders in Washington D.C. that the best way to catch an Apache was with another Apache.

Since warriors had only two ways of reclaiming the freedom they had lost, either by becoming a scout or turning renegade, it wasn't surprising that so many of them swallowed their pride and agreed to work for the Army. It was the only outlet open to them which would not result in their being hunted down like animals.

White Apache did not hold it against them, although Delgadito did. The renegade leader despised any Apache who sided with the conquerors of their people.

Rounding a bush, White Apache discovered an arroyo in front of him, running from south to north. He stepped to the rim. It did not contain water and was only four-feet deep. Jumping down, he bore to the right.

As he recollected, earlier he had crossed the arroyo about a hundred yards to the north at a point where the banks had buckled. From there he would be able to see the horse as well as his back trail and have a clear view of the chaparral on both sides.

White Apache abruptly stopped and cocked his head. The shooting had stopped and he had not even realized it. Now he could hear the sigh of the wind, but nothing else.

Keeping his head below the rim, White Apache crept past a bend. Ahead was the spot where he had crossed with the gelding. He took a few more steps, then crouched, puzzled by what appeared to be a post in the very middle of the arroyo, about twenty feet ahead. He peered at it closely. It stood three feet high and was as thin as a rail.

Cautiously, White Apache went on. Whatever that thing was, it shouldn't be there. Flash floods had long since swept any and all vegetation from the bottom of the arroyo. There weren't even any boulders or rocks.

When about three strides away, recognition caused White Apache to halt in surprise. It was a rifle! It was a Winchester like his own! Someone had wedged the stock into the soft soil so that the gun stood upright. In and of itself, the act seemed without rhyme or reason. But White Apache was not so easily deceived. There was only one person who could have done it, and one reason why that person had.

White Apache glanced to the right and left. He saw clumps of dirt at the bottom of the west bank and started to pivot but he was already too late. The bank exploded in a shower of earth. A knife glinted in the starlight as the scout rammed into him and drove him against the other side.

Clay's Winchester was sent flying. He grabbed for the warrior's knife arm but he could not get a grip. He winced as the knife dug a groove in his left side. The blade glanced off a rib, then thudded into the bank.

Seizing the scout's wrist, White Apache held fast even as he arced his knee at the warrior's groin. The man was a canny fighter; a quick twist was all he needed to deflect the knee with his hip.

Propping a foot behind him, White Apache pushed off the bank toward the middle where he would have room to maneuver. A fist caught him low in the stomach, nearly doubling him over. Apaches were not fistfighters, so clearly this one had learned a trick or two from the whites he worked with.

White Apache forked a foot behind the other's leg and shoved, seeking to unbalance his foe. But the scout gave a little hop, twisted, and hooked his own foot behind White Apache. Before White Apache could brace himself he was flat on his back with the warrior's knee on his chest and that knife inching steadily lower toward his jugular. Sweeping his left hand up, he held the other's arm at bay with both hands.

Antonio's features were contorted in feral savagery. He was going to kill this white-eye or die

163

trying. Bloodlust caused temples to pound, his veins to bulge. He was in the grip of a killing frenzy the likes of which he had only experienced once before, many years ago during a battle with Mexican soldados when his band had been trapped in a box canyon and been forced to fight their way out against overwhelming odds. That had been a glorious day, perhaps the single best day of his life. He had slain eleven Nakai-yes, four of them with his bare hands.

Now Antonio would slay the white-eye no one else could kill. Many had tried, he knew. The Army, fellow scouts, bounty hunters, lawmen, they all had failed. The glory would go to him and him alone.

Wrenching his knife arm to one side, Antonio nearly freed it. But the white-eye clung on. He had to compel Taggart to let go, so he lunged and closed his left hand on the white man's throat.

Clay jerked his neck to the right, hoping to break loose, and could not. Frantic, he bucked upward, striving to throw the scout off, without success. The warrior was a weathered veteran of more combat than Clay had ever seen. The scout knew every trick there was and anticipated his every move.

Brute force was the last resort. Whipping his body from side to side, White Apache exerted every iota of strength he had and pushed the blade back a few inches. It was not much but it would have to do.

The fingers on White Apache's neck had closed off his air and his lungs were close to bursting. He must do something, and soon, or he would pass out.

White Apache dared not let go of the warrior's arm, though, or that knife would slice into him. He knew it and the warrior knew it, and he knew that the warrior knew it. It was the very last thing the

Apache would expect. So that was exactly what he did.

Swooping his left hand to the ground at his side, White Apache scooped up a palmful of dirt even as the Bowie dipped toward him. In a twinkling he had hurled the dirt into the scout's eyes. As he did, he flipped to the left. It wasn't enough to dislodge the scout but it was enough to make the knife miss his neck by a hair and sink into the ground instead.

Antonio cried out, a gravely snarl of rage. The dirt stung terribly, blinding him, filling his eyes with tears. He tried to stab the white-eye anyway and felt the knife spear into the soil. His left hand was torn from the white man's throat. Realizing that he was vulnerable, he threw himself backward and rose, furiously wiping at his eyes.

White Apache drew his own Bowie as he stood. He could have drawn his Colt. Or he could have picked up his Winchester. But he knew enough of Apache ways to know that the scout held a personal grudge against him. There was no other explanation for the warrior attacking him with a knife when the man could just as easily have shot him from ambush. Which was fine with him. If it was personal, so be it. He would give as good as he got.

Antonio back-pedaled while blinking his eyes. He did not understand why the white-eye had not finished him off. Suddenly his vision cleared enough for him to see Taggart standing there with a knife in hand. Understanding brought a grim smile to his lips. So! This white-eye was more Apache than Antonio had given him credit for being. In his own tongue, he said, "You will soon be dead, man of pale skin. But I kill you with respect, for of all the whites I have ever met, you are the only one worthy of it."

The words were lost on Clay. He did not speak

the Jicarilla language. The smile, a rarity among Apaches, conveyed more than the words ever could. He smiled back, just as somberly, then had to parry a thrust as the warrior skipped in close with lightning speed.

Apaches were masters at knife fighting. It was yet another of the many skills they learned at an early age. Antonio was typical. He had defeated a score of adversaries with a blade, some of them fellow warriors slain after a formal challenge. His skill was exceptional, and he brought every bit of it to bear against the renegade.

Several Chiricahua warriors had instructed White Apache in how to use a knife. He had learned much but in no regard was he the equal of an Apache. In this instance he barely countered another swing, then retreated under a fierce onslaught. The two blades rang together time and again. Unexpectedly he backed into the bank and had to leap to the right as the scout speared at his chest.

In ducking under a backhand slash that would have taken his head off, White Apache tripped. He stumbled and nearly fell. The warrior seized the moment and lanced the knife toward his shoulder. Again White Apache threw himself aside but this time he was not quite fast enough and suffered a three-inch cut that flared his arm with torment and caused blood to flow freely.

Antonio, assuming that his adversary was weakening, attacked with renewed vigor. He cut low, then high. Both were blocked. He drove the crimson tip at White Apache's chest. When the renegade skipped aside, he pivoted and tried to rip the blade into the man's stomach. Once more he narrowly missed.

White Apache was mere heartbeats away from

eternity. He countered, parried, spun and dodged a blow which would have cleaved his head from hair to chin. The scout did not give him a moment's respite. He had to leap rearward or be gutted like a fish.

A frown curled the Jicarilla's thin lips. It was taking much longer than it should have. The White Apache was every bit a worthy opponent.

The Bowie whistled at White Apache's face. A pang shot up his arm as he met the knife with his own. For several moments they were locked together, nose to nose, both of them panting and grunting as they tried to knock the other down. They turned first to the right, then to the left. Neither enjoyed an edge.

Then Antonio resorted to a ruse learned long ago. He pretended to weaken. He bent backward, causing White Apache to lean forward to keep the pressure on his knife. And at the very instant when the white-eye started to lean, Antonio whirled to the left.

White Apache was caught off guard. He stumbled forward. His left foot twisted in a rut and he fell. By throwing out his right arm he kept from landing on his stomach. But in a rush of insight he realized that his back was exposed, realized that was exactly what the Apache had planned, and realized that in another moment the warrior would bury the Bowie in him and that would be the end of it.

Blocking or evading the thrust was impossible. Yet as White Apache smacked down onto his hands and knees, he happened to glance between his legs and see the scout's feet. He saw the warrior's right moccasin lift and move toward him as the man stepped in for the killing stroke. Without thinking, acting on pure reflex, White Apache slammed his own right foot to the rear, into the scout's shin. He must have caught the Apache at just the right moment because the warrior lost his balance and toppled.

Whirling and rising, White Apache firmed his grip on the knife hilt and streaked the blade at the man's throat. If his foe had been a white man, the clash would have been over right then. But the Apache was just too quick. Clay's knife nicked the side of the warrior's neck, that was all.

In a lithe bound Antonio regained his footing. He did not let on, but he was rattled by his narrow escape. In all his years, in all the fights he had been in, no one had ever come so close to rubbing him out. No one had ever given him so much trouble as this white-eye.

Antonio was beginning to see why this man had become the scourge of the territory. He was beginning to appreciate why no one had been able to kill or capture him. Clay Taggart had a natural knack for dealing death that few men, white or red, could boast of. Taggart was a born killer, as the whites would say. Yet from the fleeting hesitation Taggart showed at times, Antonio doubted the white-eye knew how formidable he truly was.

Clay Taggart was not feeling very formidable. In fact, he was feeling hopelessly outclassed. He had tried everything he could think of and nothing had worked. He had barely stayed one step ahead of the scout the whole fight. To his way of thinking it was just a matter of time before the inevitable took place. His only regret was that he would never get to take his revenge on Miles Gillett.

The very next instant, Clay stepped onto some loose dirt and his foot shot out from under him. He tried to regain his balance but it was a lost cause. His back hit the west bank and he slid lower.

Antonio had the white-eye, at last! A bound

brought him in front of the renegade. He snapped his knife on high and girded himself to plunge it down.

White Apache knew he had reached the end of his rope. He saw the knife pause at the apex of its swing and braced for the searing agony he was bound to endure when the blade sank to the hilt. Then, just when his death seemed certain, he was stunned to see the scout freeze, to see the Apache glance sharply up at the top of the bank.

A low, ominous growl sounded. Simultaneously, a squat, hairy form hurtled out of nowhere and rammed the Apache squarely in the chest. Both went down in a flurry of snapping jaws and rending claws. The warrior's knife arm straightened but the blow never landed. Those steely jaws clamped down. The crunch of bone was loud and crisp.

White Apache gawked, too astonished to move or stand. He did not know where the animal came from, or even what it was. In bewildered fascination he watched as the beast's teeth hooked into the Apache's side and tore the skin open from below the shoulder to the waist. How the warrior kept from crying out, White Apache would never know.

The scout made a valiant effort to stand. He shoved the animal from him and was halfway erect when the brute leaped. The same jaws which had shattered bone now clamped onto the base of his throat. With an almost casual toss of its shaggy head, the wolfish creature ripped the neck open.

Spurting a scarlet geyser, Antonio tottered to the rear. Strangely, the beast made no move to close in. It stood and stared as his lifeblood soaked his uniform shirt and pants and darkened the dirt underfoot. He saw it glance at the White Apache but make no move to harm him, leading Antonio to conclude that the two were in league somehow, that the beast had come to the rescue of the man. It filled him with amazement. Truly the White Apache possessed powerful medicine if so powerful a brute did his bidding. In a way it made Antonio feel less bitter. He had been defeated, but not by any ordinary man. It had taken a white witch with the power of a *Gans*.

Weakness came over Antonio, weakness such as he had never known. His legs gave way and he melted to the ground. His final sight was of the wolf-ish creature grinning at him.

Clay Taggart's skin pricked as if to a thousand needles when the wolf-dog suddenly swung toward him. He realized that he should have stood while he had the chance because now his face and his throat were at the same height as the beast's head and jaws. He thought of trying to stab it but elected to let it make the first move.

The creature took a step toward him, then stopped to raise its muzzle and sniff loudly. Again and again it inhaled, turning its head from side to side.

Clay had the impression that the beast did not know what to make of him. Perhaps because he dressed like an Indian but smelled like a white man, it was confused. He made no hostile moves as it edged nearer, still sniffing. Its black, twitching nose was mere inches from his leg when it unexpectedly whined and coiled to spring. He tensed, thinking it was about to attack. Instead, the creature leaped clear over him to the rim of the bank and was gone.

White Apache leaped up. The wolf-dog had stopped a dozen feet away and looked back as if waiting to see what he would do. On an impulse, Clay retrieved his Winchester and scrambled up the side of the arroyo. The beast was already heading westward at an even lope. He followed it, pushing himself to keep it in sight. Soon it disappeared. He was about to stop and go back when he spotted flickering flames off through the chaparral.

On cat's feet White Apache approached the campfire. Presently he halted behind a manzanita. He saw two people, a hawkish man who was oddly familiar and another with short blond hair who lay bundled in blankets, resting propped against a saddle. The hawkish man turned toward him and he noticed a pearl-handled Colt worn butt forward on the right hip. Suddenly he remembered. It was the gunman from the Triangle G. One of Gillett's gunmen. His hand tightened on the Winchester.

From out of the brush to the east walked the wolf-dog. Neither of those at the fire showed any alarm. The blond one smiled weakly, while the gunman declared, "There you are, Razor. Where the devil have you been? What did you smell out there that you took off like that?"

The beast laid down beside the man under the blankets, who then spoke in a high-pitched voice. "What do we do now, my dearest?"

White Apache started. It took him a few seconds to recognize the speaker was a woman.

The gunman poured coffee from a pot into a tin cup and took it over. "Here. This will perk you up some. But I still want you to lie there until I say differently. A shoulder wound like yours can turn serious if it gets infected."

"Whatever you say, darlin'," the woman said with a joyous grin.

"Oh, hell," the gunman said for some reason. Bending, he kissed her passionately. The embrace lingered on and on, and when they parted the woman leaned her head back and grinned dreamily.

171

"If I'd only known," she said.

White Apache did not know what to make of her comment. He studied them, debating whether to do as his Chiricahua brothers would do and slay them both.

"Before you get all misty-eyed on me," the gunman said, "we'd better decide what we're going to do. It sure doesn't make any sense to go on by ourselves, not with you wounded and all." He shifted as if nervous and gave a little cough. "I've been thinking. It seems to me that we should forget this whole business and head for Kentucky. I still have a few friends back there. And I recollect this parcel of land that I'd like to get my hands on. It's not much, but with hard work we can make something of it."

"You're forgettin' one thing. What about Gillett? What about the five thousand he's already paid?"

The gunman's grin was as sly as that of a fox. "I'm not forgetting anything. How do you reckon we'll pay for the land?" He stroked her cheek. "The way I see it, he owes you. Five thousand doesn't begin to make up for the loss of two brothers."

"Gillett won't see it that way. He'll think we stole it from him."

"Who the hell cares what he thinks?"

Clay Taggart saw the woman blink, then smile. They kissed again. Wearing a smile of his own, he melted back into the brush and headed eastward. He was not about to kill them. Anyone who would steal from Miles Gillett was no enemy of his.

Of the three near the fire, only one noticed the White Apache's departure. It wasn't the woman, who had found the love she had never known she was looking for, nor the gunman, who had found the answer to mending his shattered soul. No, it was the wolf-dog, and Razor, of course, told no one.

WHITE APACHE

Jake McMasters

Follow the action-packed adventures of Clay Taggart, as he fights for revenge against settlers, soldiers, and savages.

#5: Bloodbath. Taggart turned the ragtag band of Apache into the fiercest fighters the Southwest has ever seen. They are his army; he uses them to kill his enemies. But on a bloody raid into the stinking wastes of Mexico, some of his men rebel. Far from familiar territory, Taggart has to battle for his life, while trying to reform his warriors into a wolf pack capable of slaughtering anyone who crosses their path.
_3689-4 $3.99 US/$4.99 CAN

#6: Blood Treachery. Settlers, soldiers, and Indians alike have tried to kill the White Apache. But it will take more than brute strength to defeat the wily desperado—it will take cold cunning and ruthless deception. And when a rival chieftain sets out to betray Taggart and his fierce band, they learn that the face of a friend can sometimes hide the heart of an enemy.
_3739-4 $3.99 US/$4.99 CAN

Dorchester Publishing Co., Inc.
65 Commerce Road
Stamford, CT 06902

Please add $1.75 for shipping and handling for the first book and $.50 for each book thereafter. NY, NYC, PA and CT residents, please add appropriate sales tax. No cash, stamps, or C.O.D.s. All orders shipped within 6 weeks via postal service book rate. Canadian orders require $2.00 extra postage and must be paid in U.S. dollars through a U.S. banking facility.

Name_____

Address _____

City _____ State_____Zip_____

I have enclosed $_____in payment for the checked book(s).
Payment **must** accompany all orders.☐ Please send a free catalog.

WHITE APACHE

Jake McMasters

Follow the action-packed adventures of Clay Taggart, as he fights for revenge against settlers, soldiers, and savages.

#3: Warrior Born. Clay Taggart is used to having enemies, and after a band of bushwhackers try to string him up, it seems that everybody in the Arizona Territory is out for his scalp. But it isn't until the leader of the Apache warriors who saved him turns against Clay that he fears for his life. But no one—not a friend or a foe—will send the White Apache to Boot Hill, and anyone who takes aim at Taggart is signing his own death warrant in blood.

__3613-4 $3.99 US/$4.99 CAN

#4: Quick Killer. Taggart's quest for revenge has made settlers in the Arizona Territory fear and hate him as much as the wretched tribe of Indians who rescued him. But for every enemy Taggart blasts to Boot Hill, another wants to send him to hell. Quick Killer is half Indian, all trouble, and more than a match for the White Apache. If Taggart doesn't kill the S.O.B. quickly, he'll be nothing more than vulture bait.

__3646-0 $3.99 US/$4.99 CAN

Dorchester Publishing Co., Inc.
65 Commerce Road
Stamford, CT 06902

Jake
McMasters

Follow Clay Taggart as he hunts the murdering S.O.B.s who left him for dead—and sends them to hell!

#1: Hangman's Knot. Strung up and left to die, Taggart is seconds away from death when he is cut down by a ragtag band of Apaches. Disappointed to find Taggart alive, the warriors debate whether to kill him immediately or to ransom him off. They are hungry enough to eat him, but they think he might be worth more on the hoof. He is. Soon the white desperado and the desperate Apaches form an alliance that will turn the Arizona desert red with blood.
_3535-9 $3.99 US/$4.99 CAN

#2: Warpath. Twelve S.O.B.s were the only reason Taggart had for living. Together with the desperate Apache warriors who'd saved him from death, he'd have his revenge. One by one, he'd hunt the yellowbellies down. One by one, he'd make them wish they'd never drawn a breath. One by one, he'd leave their guts and bones scorching under the brutal desert sun.
_3575-8 $3.99 US/$4.99 CAN

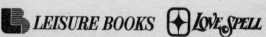